FLOUNDERING

Romy Ash lives in Melbourne. *Floundering* is her first novel.
www.romyash.com

FLOUNDERING

ROMY ASH

TEXT PUBLISHING MELBOURNE AUSTRALIA

textpublishing.com.au

The Text Publishing Company
Swann House
22 William Street
Melbourne Victoria 3000
Australia

First published in 2012 by The Text Publishing Company
Reprinted 2012, 2013

Page design by Susan Miller
Cover design by W. H. Chong
Typeset in Adobe Garamond Pro by J & M Typesetting

Printed in Australia by Griffin Press, an Accredited ISO AS/NZS 14001:2004 Environmental Management System printer

National Library of Australia Cataloguing-in-Publication entry:
Author: Ash, Romy, 1981–
Title: Floundering / Romy Ash.
ISBN: 9781921922084 (pbk.)
ISBN: 9781921834776 (eBook)
Subjects: Children of disappeared persons—Fiction.
          Mothers and sons—Fiction.
Dewey number: A823.4

For my family.

part one

1

I have that itchy skin feeling that someone is watching us. I turn around and it's Loretta. She is in a car following us slowly, like a pervert would. I'm counting letterboxes and Jordy is walking ahead 'cos he likes to pretend I'm not his brother.

Loretta waves at us to get in.

Hi, she says. Hi.

Jordy and I stand like statues. Her hair is a different colour. She looks wonky. But after a bit all her features come together and she is Loretta again. I get in the car. I don't like how Gran makes the beds. She pulls the sheet so tight that every night you got to kick and kick and kick to get it free. Jordy doesn't get in the car. I already have my seatbelt on.

He says, Where've you been?

I've come to get you, she says.

But where've you been?

I've been everywhere, man – come on, get in. I've missed you.

But you can't – and he shakes the words from his head and starts walking away.

Matey, she says, come on. She is driving really slow along-side him. He shrugs his schoolbag further up on his shoulder and stops.

She smiles the kind of smile that is so good it feels like a punch in the stomach. Jordy looks up and down the street, but there is nothing to hold on to, just letterboxes, fences and scraggly trees. He gets in.

She drums her fingers on the steering wheel, looking back at me in the rear-view mirror. Man, I've been so excited to see you.

Driving too fast. She has silver bangles that sparkle.

I was driving here, I was thinking all like, will they have grown? she says. She looks at me. You look big, she says with a wink, and laughs. I look away. On the seat there's a brush with strands of her blonde hair in it, and a discarded grey hoodie.

I got some chips. She rustles around under Jordy's legs.

He says, Hey!

She brings out a packet of Twisties. You gotta share, though, okay? She throws them on Jordy's lap.

Jordy opens them and grabs the bright yellow curls.

Can I've some? I say.

Course you can, sweet pea, she says.

Jordy takes another handful then leans over the seat with the packet. I reach my hand in deep, trying to get as many as possible in one go. When I pull my hand out Twisties go everywhere.

We're going to have so much fun. She squeals a little squeal and jiggles around in her seat. It's going to be great.

Jordy, can I've some more? I say.

He pretends like he hasn't heard me and eats a handful so big it makes his cheeks fat. Jordy, I say. He turns round and shows me the shiny inside of the empty packet. His grin is yellow. I hate you, I say.

One by one, I eat the Twisties I spilt before, picking up the yellow curls from the cracks in the seat and from the floor. I try wipe the powdery crumbs off my school shorts, but my fingers are covered in colouring and it makes it worse. I lick my fingers until they are clean, wipe my shorts again.

You guys have grown heaps, she says.

You don't have to pretend, Jesus, says Jordy. He hides behind his fringe that hangs across his face. He won't let Gran cut it, and it's straight and slick. Even if Gran let me keep my hair long too, it wouldn't hang like that. Mine always looks messy, no matter what, even after Gran has combed it and wet it down. It springs back up, like static. But he has grown, I reckon, his school shorts are too short now, even when he wears them so low I see his underpants above the band. I don't think I've grown. Gran says not to worry. She reckons I'll catch up, it's just the way it is with boys.

So why are you here anyway? Jordy says. He's looking at Loretta. His profile is sharp.

What do you mean, honey? she says and takes her eyes from the road.

How come you left us?

Hon, I never left you. I was always coming to get you.

3

Things just got complicated, is all.

But it's been, like, a year.

I know honey and I missed you two so much I thought I might die. You hear me? So much. Now, are you good? You good? She turns around and gives me a quick, concerned look before turning back to the road.

Yeah, I say. Jordy doesn't say anything, just turns away, looks out his window at the road. I wind my window down and half close my eyes – make the little white posts, the grass and the trees all blur. I do this for a long time.

Loretta doesn't ring Gran until we are right across the border into the next state.

They're with me, Mum. It's fine.

I've got a hold of Loretta's hand, and she's keeping the glass door of the phone booth open with her sneaker. I can feel Loretta's painted fingernails, two of them broken and sharp against my palm.

No, Mum, they're my boys. I'm not having this conversation with you again. They're my boys. I've got a place ready and everything. Please, Mum, she says. Don't say that. I told you already. That's why I'm ringing you now, Mum.

She's leaning her head against the glass with the orange phone curled around her face.

Loretta don't let us call her mum, says the only mum in her life is Gran and she don't want to be like Gran. I can picture Gran at the kitchen table on the new portable phone that makes it sound like you're speaking into a cave. Sometimes Loretta used to call. Sitting at the table, Jordy and I passed the phone between us.

4

Her real voice sounds so different to the one that spoke on the phone. It's warm. I hold her hand tight. She squeezes back.

I look up at Loretta, but her face is hidden behind her streaky blonde hair. Jordy's still in the car. I can see him through the phone booth door. He's in the front seat hunched over, staring at his bellybutton. The car is yellow and rusted. I name it Bert in my head.

No, it won't happen again, not like last time. I'm good, Mum. I'm so good right now.

I can't hear what Gran is saying but Loretta's voice gets loud and high. No, I'm not telling you where. I know you won't do it. Don't bring police into this, Mum, they're my boys. They can't do nothing. Don't threaten me. Mum. They're my boys. No, Mum, I'm not speaking to Dad. Mum. Mum.

Loretta clangs the phone down hard. Fuck, she says, fuck. She tugs my hand, wipes her face on the shoulder of her hoodie and pulls me outside. She's breathing deep breaths and it's like she's forgotten I'm standing there. But she's got my hand gripped so tight it hurts.

Loretta?

What? she says angrily. When she looks down at me, she forces a smile and once it's been there for a while it settles and looks like a real one. What? she says, nicer this time – her skinny, plucked eyebrows up in the air.

You're hurting my hand.

Ha. Sorry, she says. But she doesn't let go, just loosens her grip. She makes me so mad, Tommo, she says.

Loretta swings my hand. The sun is setting over the service station.

She makes me crazy even, she says and laughs. But it's okay

5

because I got you, don't I.

She swings my arm high, pulls me towards the servo doors. They open automatic, like a welcome.

Let's get some chips, eh.

Can I've salt and vinegar?

Sure you can, honey, she says. It's like she never swore or was angry, it's erased already.

Standing in the line behind a big man whose gut hangs all the way over his pants, Loretta's turning the sunglasses rack. Her hoodie slung off one bony shoulder. She picks out two wrap-around pairs and squats down in front of me.

Put these on, she says. The servo goes dark. Perfect, she says. You're going to need these, she says and pulls them off my face. She tickles me and I squeal and try to escape. It's not until we're outside that I realise there's a pair of sunnies in each of my pockets. As we walk towards the car the top of the phone booth lights up. It's bright and orange and shining like a beacon.

Jordy says to us from out of the dark, What took you so long?

How's this look? Loretta says and pulls into a rest stop, parking behind some trees. There's a sign in the headlights that says Survive The Drive. Jordy, half asleep on a pillow against the window, looks up and says, Whatever.

I say, Loretta, I'm hungry.

She turns around to look at me, We'll get some brekkie in the morning. Let's just have some kips now, hey.

Are we going to sleep here?

Yep. It's a rest stop, you know, for rest.

She turns the headlights off and the world goes dark. She

gets out. I hear the boot open and close, then she opens my side door and chucks a blanket on me.

There you go, poppet, she says and walks off into the darkness. My heart beats fast as she's walking away. I want to call out to her, but I know it's stupid, so I just hold my breath. I start counting in my head, think if she gets back by one hundred it'll be okay. A semi-trailer passes and it lights her up: squatting down, arms resting on her knees, bum bare, pissing. Next to her is a bin overflowing with rubbish. The rumble of the truck shakes the car and then it's gone. I stop counting, but lock the doors.

The day Loretta left us with Gran and Pa she just dropped us on their front doorstep in our board shorts, with beach towels around our shoulders. We dripped two pools of brown water from the coca-cola lake, where Loretta had taken us swimming. She waved goodbye like we was just going for a visit and she'd be back in a couple of hours to pick us up. They lived on the coast, way south of the city. The glass in the front door had frosted seagulls flying across it. I had a Bubble O' Bill in my hand and it melted pink and blue. I couldn't picture what Gran looked like because we hadn't seen her since we were littler. Since the last time Loretta had left us at Gran's and then come back. That time Loretta had met us at the river and we ate fish and chips on a wooden table. The chips fat and thick as men's fingers. Gran and Loretta had argued and Loretta pulled us into the car – a different one to Bert – before I had time to eat my potato scallop.

When Gran opened the door she looked like any old lady.

Gran? Jordy said.

7

Jordy, she said and sighed.

Before I went in I made sure I could see some mixed-up bits of Loretta in her, 'cos what if Loretta had put us on the wrong doorstep? Gran sat us at the kitchen table, pulled the ice-cream from my hand and dumped it in the sink. Wiped my hand roughly with a chequered tea towel. She got us both a plastic cup of green cordial. She looked at Jordy. Jordy looked at me and I looked at the tablecloth. It was plastic with a rose pattern.

Where's your mother? she said.

Pa came in the back door. He had two fish, his fingers hooked up through their slashed throats and into their mouths. His fingertips resting on sharp, little teeth. He raised his eyebrows at the lot of us.

When did they turn up? Gran didn't answer. Loretta?

Gran shook her head, No, love.

Pa breathed a big breath inside himself then let it out. They better be on their best behaviour, he said.

Hush, they're good kids.

He gutted them fish in the sink with my ice-cream. The warm insides of the fish melted the ice-cream until there was only the bubblegum nose left. The guts went into two plastic bags and then into the freezer. He washed his hands with hard soap from a little dish above the sink then sat down across from us. He had blue eyes, same as Loretta. It felt weird to have them looking at us from his old man leathery face. Gran had a ham and chutney sandwich ready for him. It was cut into two triangles. She set it in front of him. I like them cut like that. He bit into the soft white bread and it made such a clean round bite I could see the marks from each tooth. I started to cry. Gran went

8

to the fridge, got out a Tupperware container, a jar of yellow homemade chutney and bread from the breadbox. She made us a sandwich each. Cut it into triangles. When they weren't looking I got the bubblegum ball from the sink. Later when we was in bed, I wiped the fish blood off and chomped through the hard shell. Blew skin-pink bubbles that burst all over my face. I blew them bubbles right through the night 'cos Loretta didn't come back to pick us up.

I hear Jordy's breathing change. I lean over the seat and look down at him. His legs are curled up. He's a ball of arms and legs. I stretch out my blanket and it's big enough to push a corner between the front seats and over Jordy.

Loretta looms at Bert's driver-side window, face white and round as a full moon. She tries to open the door and taps on the window for me to let her in. I pull the lock up. She slips in the car.

You locking me out, are you? she says.

No, I say and look out at the trees that light up tall and white in the headlights of another truck.

She locks her door again and winks at me. Just in case, she says. She's in the front seat with her hoodie for a blanket. I open the window a slit to let the stink of us out. I'm busting to do a wee, but I can hear the rustling of monsters out there.

I can't sleep, Loretta.

Whatcha talking about?

I can't sleep.

Shut up, Jordy hisses from the front seat.

I can't sleep, I whisper. Pulling the blanket right up to my chin and feeling the scratchy wool against my lips. The blanket smells of dog. Jordy tugs on the other end of it.

When'd you have a dog? I go.

I didn't have a dog, she says. Shhh.

But I can smell a dog.

Just where I was staying, sweets, it wasn't my dog.

At your house?

Yeah, at my house.

Can we get a dog?

Just go to sleep, okay.

But I can't sleep, Loretta.

Tom.

I grip the corner of the blanket tight. And it's only in the morning, with the windows steamed up, and wee cramping my stomach that I realise I've fallen asleep.

Shotgun, says Jordy. He's leaning against the passenger side door.

What? I go. You had shotgun all yesterday. It's my turn.

I called it.

But it's my turn.

There's no turns, I called it. If you wanna sit shotgun, you gotta call it. He's sniggering at me from behind his fringe. He flicks it off his face and gives me a slippery smile. If you call it, I'll let you have a go.

I look around for Loretta but she's over near a slack wire fence that's supposed to keep us from a dusty paddock. There's brown sheep out there looking weighed down by their woolly coats. She's blowing smoke out into nothing. I turn back to Jordy – we're still in our school uniforms, he's crumpled, his blue school shorts hanging above his knobbly knees. I put my arms out in front of me and make two fists and start whirling them around like windmills.

Jordy, I'm just going to walk forward, and if you happen to get in the way, then it's not my fault, I'm just walking, minding me own business.

I walk towards him. He rolls his eyes at me. I clench my hands as hard as I can and aim for his face. I get one in before he has two of my wrists in one of his hands. I start kicking him, aiming for his balls. But he has me on the ground, with my face in the dirt, and his knee digging deep in my back before I can get him in the nuts. I can't see his face, only the rubbish blowing from the overflowing bin. He gets off me. I feel weightless.

If you call it, you can have it, you just got to call it, he says.

I sit up and try brush the dirt off my school uniform. Jordy's leaning against the passenger door.

It's totally fair, he says.

Loretta's walking back. I hear her silver bangles before I see her. She drops her cigarette butt.

Loretta, can I've shotgun?

Loretta looks at us both. Who called it?

Jordy just laughs and gets in the front seat. Loretta shrugs and I'm still there kneeling in the dirt. The wind blows the smell from the bin.

My stomach grumbles so loud it's definitely talking to me. We pull up at a servo. I put my scuffed black school shoes on with no socks, because the asphalt is already too hot to walk on with bare feet. They feel too small, my toes push against the leather. I shake the stiffness out of my legs. I look up at the Shell sign, poking into a sky so blue I can imagine it's the ocean.

What are you looking at, dipshit? says Jordy, slapping me on the back of the head.

None of your beeswax, I say and go stand near the front passenger door of the car. I can see the blonde of Loretta's head through the dusty windows of the servo. There's tinsel strung on the inside, hanging in arches. Gran had put up a plastic Christmas tree in the corner of the lounge room. She hung it with silver snowflakes and fairy lights that flickered on and off. The cards from all her friends, hung on a string across the front window, blew off every afternoon when the wind turned onshore.

Shotgun, I say and look triumphantly over at Jordy.

Nah, he says, you've got to call it in the morning. I've got shotgun for the rest of the day.

I called it, Jordy, I say.

Nah, you've got to call it in the morning.

That's not fair. You said if I call it I can have it.

Yeah, if you call it in the morning, you can have it. It's totally fair.

I look around for Loretta. She's walking fast towards the car.

Get in the car, she says from still far away.

But Mum, Jordy won't let me have a go. The mum slips out of me, strange in my mouth.

Get in the car.

She's wrenching on her door and then she is in the front

seat. Jordy pushes me out of the way and gets shotgun fast. Loretta starts the engine.

Get in.

I open the back door and have to jump in as she accelerates. I close the door, watching the tar blurring in the open bit before I can get it shut. I fumble for my seatbelt and click it in. Safe.

Loretta pulls two pies in plastic sachets from inside her hoodie. Breakfast, she says and chucks one back to me. The pie lands on my leg, burns my bare skin. I pick it up by a plastic corner. It hangs inside it, steam coming out the little plastic holes.

Thanks, I say.

Don't be rude, she goes.

You burned my leg.

What'd I say? Don't be rude. Looking at me in the rearview. Yesterday she looked neat but today her eyes are all smudged black. She looks away from me, and I look out the window. The paddocks go past, the same as before. I put the pie down on the seat beside me and wait for it to cool. Little flakes of pastry inside the bag look as thin and gross as flakes of skin. I start kicking the back of Jordy's seat.

Hot, isn't it, says Loretta.

She tries to get her hoodie off. She is holding the steering wheel with one hand and trying to inch the jumper off with the other. I'm so sweaty my legs are sticking to the seat. I move around to try and unpeel them.

Jordy, can you hold this for a sec?

He looks at her, Really?

Just hold it steady, hey.

Jordy leans over the gearstick and grabs hold of the wheel with two hands, his pie, half eaten, like a big brown smile, resting on the dash. Loretta has her left arm out and is wriggling her right when I look up and notice we're on the wrong side of the road.

I see the sun reflecting off the windscreen of a car driving straight for us, a bright star of light. I think of the star of Bethlehem, 'cos I was learning the Christmas carol about it for the end-of-year school performance. I see Loretta look up and take her foot off the accelerator. Jordy takes his hands off the wheel and no one's holding it for a second. The car beeps a long beep at us and Loretta grabs the wheel and swerves at the last second. Her hoodie hangs off the end of her arm, forgotten.

I look over at the car as it passes and I can see the woman driving. Her face is a cartoon drawing of frightened.

Shit, says Loretta. We almost come to a stop. There is nothing now, no cars behind us or in front of us. Are you stupid? Do you want to get us killed?

He just looks at her, not saying nothing.

So fuck–ing stupid, she says and shakes her head so that for a moment her hair goes everywhere. She bangs the steering wheel. Stupid, stupid, stupid.

Jordy looks away and I touch the back of his shoulder. He shrugs my hand off. His pie has fallen into his lap.

Loretta looks up and I see the fan of freckles across her nose and cheeks. And all over her skin tiny drops of sweat. She accelerates until we're going fast again. Jordy scoops the pie out of his lap and flings it out the window. I stick my head out, and have a look and there's a brown streak of meat down the side of Bert. Out at the edges of the paddock I see a dead eagle slung

on a wire fence. No one says anything. I savour my pie, eating it
so slowly that by the time I'm done it's cold.

Hey, look, says Loretta.

Jordy is leaning against his door, his back to Loretta, chin
resting near the open window.

Look, she says and slows the car down a little. Salt lakes.

What? I say. Loretta catches my eye in the rear-view and
gives me a smile. She pulls off the road going too fast still, and
rocks ping off Bert's belly. Jordy starts and sits up, gives Loretta
a look that makes me shrink down in my seat. She stops the car
and I jolt into the seatbelt.

Through my open window and past a wire fence the air
looks liquid. I push the door, popping it open with my shoulder.
The sun gets me like the worst kind of hug. Tiny flowers squeeze
out from a crack in the dirt and I can see a long line of ants
heading to the salt. A little bird is holding like crazy to a stalk
of grass. I turn back and look at Loretta, and she's picking at
a pimple on her arm, still in Bert. Jordy's sitting there, eyes to
the front.

I'm going to look, I say and scuff my school shoes in the
dirt. She stares up at me, and through the window I see that
her arms are covered in tiny scabs. She puts her hand in the
bit between the seats, finds a pair of sunnies from the servo.
She chucks them in Jordy's lap, and gets out of the car. Hers
wrap right around her face. I finger mine in my pocket – shiny,
smooth – and put them on.

Let's look, she says.

I climb down into the ditch beside the road. It's filled with
rubbish, broken bottles. Hot grass scratches my calves. I slip

through the barbed wire fence. I walk towards the edge of the lake, but it's not as close as it looks from the car and halfway out there it's too hot and I want to turn around.

When I look back Loretta is caught on the wire. Her arms are outstretched and struggling. Jordy climbs through and doesn't help her. His eyes are black with the sunglasses, and after this I don't see him take them off for what seems like forever. He walks out towards me.

When we get to the salt it's dirty pink and crusty under my feet. Jordy crunches onto it beside me. He picks at the meat pie on his school shorts.

I lean over, crack a piece of the salt with my fingers and put it in my mouth. It tastes like potato chips.

Jordy copies me: picks at a bit of salt, puts it in his mouth. He looks at me, spits it out.

It tastes like dirt, he says.

Loretta comes over. She has a long scratch on her thigh. It's nasty red. She touches it absently.

How hot is it? she says.

Jordy turns to Loretta, the salt cracking around his feet. Why'd we have to run anyway?

Run where, hon? she says.

From the servo.

We didn't run, honey, she says and goes to tousle his hair. He pulls away from her and she's left with just one strand. It shines for a moment in the sun.

Whatever, he says and stalks back to the car. I rub the toe of my shoe in the salt.

I'm hot, I say to Loretta and look up at her.

Come on, she says, putting her hand on my shoulder. She gives me a little squeeze. We walk back to Bert. Jordy is in the front, staring straight ahead again. I yank the door open and crawl into the back seat. My mouth is dry and my legs are scratched and stinging. There's the end of a bottle of Coke on the floor. I sip it and it's as hot as tea.

2

This'll do, eh? says Loretta.

Are we going in there? says Jordy.

The town is dark, except for squares of blue television light in house windows. Only the pub is open and a Chinese restaurant that has lace curtains and a red dragon painted across the glass. Loretta parks in front of the pub.

Yeah, says Loretta, you hungry? Jordy doesn't say anything. Are you hungry? she says to me in the rear-view.

Yeah, I say, I want to go to the Chinese. But then I want to bite my words back into my mouth because Jordy looks at me and his face makes me feel sick.

Yeah, she says, that's where we're going.

Stepping out of the hot stink of Bert, my skin goose pimples. The night's not cold, but it's dark and the darkness makes it feel cold. Jordy's still got his sunnies on, he pushes them to the top of his head. They hold his fringe back and his face looks foreign and exposed, his forehead too white. Loretta has the boot open and is rifling through a suitcase. She pulls her singlet off, leaning half into the boot. I see a sunburn-edged white cross on her back from the straps. X marks the spot. She slips a jumper over it.

You cold? she says.

I shake my head, looking at a red dress that's fallen out of the suitcase and onto the dusty bumper. There's cowboy boots in there and a paperback with its cover ripped off.

You sure?

I nod.

She slams the boot shut. Come on then, she says and walks across the wide, empty street to the light. She opens the restaurant door. A bell tinkles.

The three of us stand there for a moment. It feels weird to see them in the bright fluoros of the restaurant. Loretta and Jordy's faces are sunburnt. We all look dirty. Loretta rakes her hands through her hair. It looks greasy and lank around her face. I don't know what I look like, but my school shoes are dusty. I try to wipe one with the top of the other but it makes it worse.

Good evening, a boy says. He's in his school uniform too – and for a second I don't feel so bad. Take a seat, he says. The restaurant is empty. He gestures to all the tables. He's slim, with bowl-cut hair.

Loretta sits at the big table with the lazy Susan on the top.

I love these, she says with a smile that makes her face look different. She looks like the only picture Gran and Pa have of her on their mantle. It's a picture of her in a school sports uniform. She's got a second-place ribbon pinned to her chest and her hair in the highest ponytail on her head, she's smiling and her freckles stand out. She looks like that. We sit down. The boy brings us menus, setting them neatly in front of us. Jordy and Loretta are far away across the white paper tablecloth.

Get whatever you want, Loretta says. Jordy looks across at me, and I refuse to look back. I'm rubbing my feet together under the table. The menu is divided into types of meat. I look at everything and try to find the cheapest thing.

Anything? I say.

Yeah, says Loretta, why not. I see Jordy roll his eyes at her. Loretta notices, but she doesn't say anything. Instead she puts her hand out and spins the lazy Susan and laughs. The soy sauce bottle slides a little and I put my hand out to slow the spin.

The boy comes back with a white pad.

Can I get you any drinks? he says.

You guys want a Coke? Three Cokes, she says, not waiting for our answer.

The boy carries the wine glasses away from the table two by two. I guess he'd be Jordy's age, the boy. A Chinese man with an apron on comes out to have a look at us. Wipes his hands on his front, then disappears.

So what do you reckon? she says, and winks. This winking is a new thing, she never winked before.

I dunno, I say. Is that your dad? I ask the boy.

Yeah, he says.

Stop being a weirdo, Jordy hisses across the table at me.

I'm not being a weirdo.

I want Mongolian lamb, says Jordy to the boy and closes

his menu with a snap. I look anywhere but the menu. The fairy lights on the Christmas tree in the corner choose this moment to come on. They flash slow, then too fast.

Tom? she says. Pick a meal.

I dunno, I say and shake my head quickly, close my menu too. Where's the toilet?

Out back, says the boy.

I scrape my chair.

Loretta screws her nose up, then smiles, We'll have the Mongolian lamb, the lemon chicken, sweet and sour pork.

Fried rice? says the boy.

For sure.

Yes, Miss.

I walk away. Inside the bathroom it's pink as a mouth and holding the heat of the day. There are dusty plastic flowers in a little vase beside the sink – red and white roses. I don't really need to wee but I concentrate and dribble into the pink toilet bowl. I press flush, then wash my hands. I use the squeezy soap. I smell them and they still smell of meat pie beneath the metallic flower scent. I wash them again and splash my face. Wipe it on a paper towel. The towel gets a smudge of my face on it. I scrunch it up and throw it in the bin. I look at myself in the mirror and try see which bits of me look like Loretta, but the only bits that do are the freckles that look like dirt.

I sit back down at the table. Jordy and Loretta aren't talking. Jordy has torn the edge of the paper tablecloth into little pieces and the bits are all around him.

So you two got girlfriends? Loretta says.

No, I say.

Jordy says, What do you reckon?

Only asking, she says.

I start tearing little pieces off the tablecloth too.

Do you have a boyfriend? Jordy says.

Don't be cheeky.

Only asking.

What about Dad? I say.

Hey, what is this? Twenty questions?

The boy comes back to the table carrying a sizzling plate and the lemon chicken. He puts them down and goes back for more. The sauce on the lemon chicken is as yellow as a kid's drawing of the sun.

I don't remember much about our dad. Jordy remembers but he won't tell me anything – like Dad is a secret he gets to keep. I know he smelt of surfboard wax and then cigarettes and poo – 'cos he smoked on the toilet. Sometimes when I smell them things I get this vision of his bare arms and the feel of stubble on my cheek. But I can't picture his face.

Loretta pushes the Susan and the dishes swing around too quickly.

Give us your bowls then, she says and we pass them to her. She gives each bowl a spoonful of rice. It covers the dragon that's biting its own tail at the bottom of my bowl. I swing the Susan so that the chicken is near me and get a big spoon of it, dripping a glob of yellow on the tablecloth.

Is everything alright? The man comes and stands tall and slim next to us.

Yeah, mate, says Loretta, no problem. She doesn't look at his face, stares at the table.

I watch him walk back to the kitchen. The boy is sitting behind the counter. He looks at me and we both look away at the same time.

What's his problem? Loretta hisses at us from her side of the table, spooning chunks of meat and pineapple into her bowl. I pick the tiny prawns from my rice and leave them on the edge, little pink c's.

Hey, Loretta says, snapping her fingers at the boy. I changed my mind, she says, I'll have a beer. Okay?

The boy brings a beer, drops of water on it, and places it carefully on a napkin. I look at her as she takes a sip and she says, What?

Nothing.

I don't like it when she drinks because it makes her heavy, and when she says my name it comes out slurred. I look away and I eat until I can see the dragon again, then I white him out with rice. Loretta gets up and goes and leans over the counter to talk to the boy. She comes back and scrapes the last of the rice and Mongolian lamb into her bowl. I feel sick.

This is nice, she says.

The boy comes and piles our plates and bowls on top of one another and takes them away. There is a perfect white circle of tablecloth where my bowl was.

Thanks, I say to the boy.

The lights dim, so the flash of the Christmas tree lights goes light, dark, light, dark. The carols are stopped and the boy walks out carrying a plate with a banana fritter and ice-cream with a single candle in it. The man follows him out and they sing, Happy birthday to you, happy birthday to you – Loretta joins in, but Jordy just looks at me – Happy birthday, dear

Tom, happy birthday to you. Hip, hip hoorah, hip, hip hoorah. Loretta is giggling and clapping.

The boy puts the plate in front of me and retreats.

Blow it out, says Loretta. Make a wish.

I don't blow it out.

Make a wish, make a wish, make a wish.

I blow and wish for a new bike, 'cos we left our ones at Gran's. The lights come back on.

It's not my birthday, though.

Well, I missed ya last one, didn't I?

It looks like a dick and balls, says Jordy.

For my eleventh birthday I had a UFO birthday cake with green icing and the shining alien lights on the cake were different-coloured lollies – so cool. Gran made it. This year, when Jordy turned thirteen he was all, I don't want a cake. But even old people in old people's homes have birthday cakes.

Well, if you're not going to eat it, says Jordy.

I'm eating it, I say and crack the fried banana's batter. Loretta leans right the way across the table and steals a bite. I swing my legs under the table – the banana is hot in my mouth, and the ice-cream cold.

Can I've a bite?

Give your brother a bite.

But he didn't give me any Twisties.

I did give you some, dipshit.

But you didn't give me an equal amount.

Are you retarded?

It *is* his birthday, Jordy. She licks icing sugar off her lips.

We'll do your birthday another night.

Jordy stands up and stalks to the bathroom. I eat it all, even though I'm so full I want to vomit.

The boy brings the bill and Loretta stares at it a long time. My heart starts beating too fast, and I look around for Jordy, hoping he gets back real quick. I push my chair out, so I'll be ready.

You going too? says Loretta.

No. I grab on to the edge of the chair.

She gets up and takes her card to the counter. I can see the boy doing his homework. I've lost count of the days, but it has to almost be school holidays. Jordy comes back and when the boy stands up to serve Loretta I see that Jordy and him are exactly the same height. They look eye to eye. Jordy walks past and out the door. It chimes cheerfully.

Sayonara, says Loretta as we leave. At least the chinks make good food, eh, she says to me as the door swings shut behind us. We're out on the empty street. The yellow of Bert down the street makes me smile. Jordy's waiting there.

Loretta unlocks the car and gets in, leaning over to unlock our doors. Jordy gets in, but I'm standing in the dark still. You're not supposed to drive after drinking, Loretta, I say.

I had one beer, thank you very much, Tom.

Have you seen that ad on telly?

I'm not talking about this.

The one where the family ends up dead and the dad cries?

I'm not talking about this, Tom. Get in.

Loretta drives a little way out of town and pulls up out

the back of a roadhouse. There are cement picnic tables. It's night, but I can't imagine anyone sitting here with their thermos, ever.

3

I'm the last to wake up. The air smells of petrol and hot chips. There are semi-trailers lined up. I press a bubble of rust in Bert's paint and my finger pushes right through.

What are you doing? Loretta says, I've got a table.

Nothing. Just looking.

Well, come on, breakfast.

I reach to take Loretta's hand and she starts to swing our arms, like she won't hold my hand if it isn't a game. I pull away.

So whatcha going to get? she says.

I look up at her and she seems way up high, her hair silhouetted against the morning sun. I think maybe there'll be a time when I'm taller than her, and she'll look up at me.

Nothing, I say.

I'm going to have fruit toast. I love truck-stop fruit toast, it's like, thick as a brick, and with the best salty butter. You want a piece of my toast?

Nah, I say.

You sure?

I shrug my shoulders.

Okay, fruit toast for all. Jordy, she swings around calling for him. Jordy. Her voice seems to hang in the air and then disappear. The road is there, like someone has got a big black Texta and a ruler, and just drawn it on the pale dirt.

I need to do a wee, I say.

We walk towards the glass doors and they open for us. Jordy's inside, kind of staring into space. Loretta goes towards the counter and I go and touch Jordy on his sleeve.

What? he says, angry but also like he's surprised to find himself standing there in the middle of the room. He walks off towards Loretta. I follow the signs to the toilet and when I open the door there is a giant man at the trough. He seems as wide as he is tall. I slip past him and lock myself into the cubicle. I just stand in there. I hear him clear his throat and spit. I wait until he's gone before I wee into the dirty toilet bowl.

Jordy, give Tom some of your chips.

I scrape the chair back and sit down. Jordy slides the basket of chips towards me. I eat one and it's cold and soft. The oil coats the inside of my mouth. I cringe. Jordy laughs.

We should hit the road, Jack. Loretta drops her crust on the plate. All her crusts are there, brown curls of them nibbled to their edges.

Gran makes us eat all our crusts.

Gran's not here, honey bunch. Her chair scrapes loudly as

she pushes it back. We all walk to the car.

I'm bored, I say and start kicking the back of Jordy's seat. I'm bored, I'm bored, I'm bored, I'm bored, I'm bored, I'm bored, I'm bored – with each kick. Loretta gives me a smile that's more a grimace and I kick harder. I decide I'll kick it for the whole day. The sun inches towards me until I'm scrunched up in a small section of shade. I swap legs and keep kicking.

Why don't you play I-spy? says Loretta.

Jordy unclicks his seatbelt and turns around.

Stop kicking my seat.

No, I say and keep the rhythm of my kicks.

He leans his long arm over and slaps me hard on the side on my head and for a moment everything goes quiet.

I'm deaf, I scream. I'm deaf.

Jordy turns back to the front and ignores me. I smash the back of his seat with both legs.

I'm deaf, I'm deaf, I'm deaf.

He leans back around and punches my legs as I kick. Shut up, he says and tries to get me in the fleshy bit of my calf.

You shut up, I say.

You're not deaf.

I am so.

You two wanna cause an accident?

You two wanna cause an accident? mimics Jordy and I watch Loretta swallow and jut her jaw out. I catch a vision of myself in the mirror and my face is red and streaked with tears. I hadn't realised I was crying. I wipe my face on my school shirt and the smell of me is gross. I look around the floor of the car for some water but there are only empty bottles around my feet.

I'm thirsty, I say and they don't say anything. I forget to keep kicking.

It means treeless plain in Aboriginal, I say, I read it on the thing.

Whatever, says Jordy.

Well, there aren't any trees. Have you got eyes? Look. We've been driving for ages.

A little bit longer, says Loretta.

I need a drink.

Well, Tom, you've got to wait. Do you see a shop? We need to wait until we get to a shop.

She gets her cigarettes, taps one out of the packet and lights up, cupping the cigarette and her face, leaning over the steering wheel. We swerve a little and I grip the armrest, hard. She breathes smoke in and out. She rights Bert on the road. Taps ash into the rusty ashtray.

Look, says Loretta, we'll stop here. She swerves off the bitumen onto the gravelly side road. There's a sign with a camera on it. She stops. The dust settles.

There's no tap, I say.

Well – so? she says. Why don't you take a look out there?

She gets out and leans on the bonnet, smoking her cigarette.

I go stand on the dirt. There's a little bird in the grass, a finch. I can tell it's a finch because Pa breeds them. It sees me and flies away. In their backyard, Pa has a long cage of finches, takes up pretty much the whole yard. The birds are all caged in sections, prize birds, breeding pairs, then the useless ones that aren't the right colours and that. They woke me up every morning – screech, screech, screech. The cages are right near

30

our bedroom window, so close you can even hear the flapping of their wings when it's quiet.

The first morning I woke up early at Gran and Pa's. I went out to look at them finches. There was one dead there, on the bottom of the cage. I opened the door, leaned in and looked at it. The other birds went fluttery. The dead one had poos on it. I picked it up. The feathers felt slippery and cool and it was small as my hand. I closed the cage quickly and took the bird back to our room.

Jordy was asleep, all in one corner of his bed. Our beds and covers matched and there was matching gold lamps that turned on when you tapped the base. Later Gran put up a dinosaur poster, but then there was only a watercolour picture of the beach, washed out up there on the wall. Pa painted them, always the same beach over and over again. I put the bird under the bed, wrapped in a tissue. The bird stank for a while, but one day when I looked it was gone and Gran never said nothing about it.

I can't see any more birds here, just the grass that's patchy right the way to the edge of the cliff. There are no fences or nothing. Just a sign saying BEWARE and a picture of a crumbly cliff and a stick figure man falling into nothing. Loretta's still leaning on the car, blowing smoke. The cliff is way up above the ocean. It looks like solid ground but in the picture it is pancake thin, the guts blown out from under it. Jordy walks out to the edge.

Look, Tom, he yells back at me. He's thin as the stick man. His shorts billow in the wind.

I walk a little way, stepping around the scrubby bushes.

Look, he says, leaning over the edge.

31

I step a little further, but the closer I get the louder the blood rushes into my ears. I look at the ground. The dirt around my feet is grey as chalk.

Look, he says. The edge is so close.

I feel dizzy.

Look. He grabs me by the arm and points down to the waves that are throwing white into the air. Way down there the rocks look the shiniest black. I can't feel my feet. Jordy grabs a hold of my other arm and steps back a little. He pushes me closer to the edge but hangs on to my arms, so for a moment it's just my toes touching the earth and the rest of me is out there, over the edge, the chalky dirt crumbling.

Saved ya life, he yells and yanks me back. I stumble onto my bum. My heart is pumping blood to every single bit of my body, even my fingertips are pulsing with it.

I hate you, I say. I hate you, and I grab a clump of dirt to fling at him. He flinches, but the wind takes it away and none of it hits him. He's laughing in chuckles that seem to burst out of him like hiccups.

What are you doing? Loretta says. She's suddenly there, her hair blowing up and around her head. She grabs us both by our school shirts. You shouldn't be near the edge. She's pulling me along the ground, so that the rocks are digging into me, and my shorts are coming down.

Stop, I say, you're hurting me. She's got a hold of Jordy too, and there's all three of us on the edge of the cliff.

Stop it, says Jordy and pulls from her grip, you're hurting him.

Loretta lets me go and I shuffle back into my shorts. A gull, catching the wind, flies up and hangs right in front of us not flapping its wings. I look off into the blue that seems brighter here than anywhere. A shadow falls on us.

You kids shouldn't – oh, the man says, oh – I thought you were kids. I didn't realise – his words hang in the air like the gull.

Pardon me? says Loretta and Gran sneaks out of her mouth.

The man blushes like a girl, from his neck right to the top of his head. Sorry, he says. He runs his hands through a thick head of grey hair. I didn't mean anything – he looks back towards his caravan, parked near Bert, and his wife is there with her arms crossed. His wife has short grey hair, they all do. Like it's impossible to grow old with long hair.

Because the sky's low with Loretta's silence he says, Where you headed?

I get up. Loretta pulls us in front of her. West, mate, we're headin' west, she says.

Well, nice to meetcha, he says and after standing there awkward, picks his way through the clumps of grass back to the caravan.

It's enormous, I say, I bet it's got a toilet in there, and a kitchen and a shower and everything.

They're carrying their poo around with them, says Jordy.

Nosey parker, Loretta says quietly to his back. Where'd they come from anyway? What are you two lookin at? She ruffles my hair and it catches in her silver rings, pulls.

Ow, I say.

When she tries to get Jordy he dodges her hand.

Don't, he says. He walks back to the car.

The couple are back in their caravan. I can see them talking through the windscreen, like the telly with the sound off. They're arguing. They don't even stop long enough to make a cup of tea. They indicate back out onto the empty highway. The gull is still there, hovering over nothing.

Loretta crouches down in front of me, You look terrible, she says, and for a second I see her forehead crease into wrinkles, but then she smiles and tries to neaten my hair. It doesn't catch this time.

Back in Bert we're driving fast towards the sun. I can feel the little scratches on my lower back. I lick my finger and rub them. I look – there's no blood. Not even a scab, but it stings with the spit. I try to nestle into the seat. Wrappers crunch under my feet.

I rest my head against the glass and it vibrates my brain. I shake my head, shake the vibrations out my ears. I see the shine of sunlight on a car by the side of the road. It's the white and blue of police and another car with all its luggage out, as if it has vomited its guts up.

Shit. Get down, says Loretta. Jordy and I look at her. I feel slow from the hours and hours of doing nothing. Get down, she yells at us. She pushes on Jordy's shoulder. Get down.

I scrunch down in the seat but too late. As we pass them I see the faces of two teenage boys, pale and wide-eyed, with long hair blowing into tails. The police officer standing there with his face in shadow under his hat. They could be brothers, them boys. Now all I can see out the window is blue sky. Get down, she says.

Stop touching me, says Jordy.

Get down, she says it softly, almost to herself.

No.

The seat is rough against my cheek. It smells of off orange juice – like a school bag.

What's the matter? I say.

Nothing, nothing's the matter.

Can I get up now?

Yep.

I look out the back window and we're heaps past them already. There are no cars behind us. No one chasing us.

You gotta do what I say, alright? she says.

I hear Jordy sigh.

Alright?

Yeah, I say.

You too, mister, she says to Jordy. But he's staring out the window like it's the most interesting thing he's ever seen, not the same stuff we've been looking at for hours and hours. We come to a border. There's just a big sign saying Farewell. On the other side there's one that says Welcome. There's a giant service station.

Now can we get a drink? I say.

4

What's wrong?

Shhhh, she says.

It's dark. We are all silent and Bert putt-putts – the engine cutting in and out. The highway is running slower beneath us. Loretta tries to pull over but when Bert stops dead we're still half on the road. Loretta has her hands on the steering wheel, she looks sideways at Jordy. It's so quiet now. The engine makes little ticking sounds. I wind my window all the way down. The desert smells nice. Bert's headlights make the bushes look flat, like cardboard.

Guess we stop here, says Loretta and then she giggles. The laugh sounds wrong, too high. We gotta get this baby off the road – out you pop, both of you. I hear Jordy sigh. I open Bert's door. The three of us stand together out there, looking at Bert.

We just have to push it a little bit off the road, says Loretta.
Jordy, you drive.

No, he says.

Tom, you drive.

I look up at her in the dark. You don't have to actually drive, you just got to steer the car while Jordy and I push it a little. It'll only be for a second.

Okay.

Get in the front.

It feels funny to open the driver's door. I get into the seat and the steering wheel is far away. I can touch it with my arms stretched out straight.

Perfect, she says. She leans over me and fiddles with the gearstick. She turns the wheel a little to the left. She positions my hands. Okay, so hold it there – eight o'clock, twelve o'clock – and we'll be just fine, she says. She closes the door. I want to hang my arm out the window, like Loretta does, but I don't. I hold tightly to the wheel, it's warm and sweaty under my palms.

Just hold it steady, Tommo, she yells at me and quieter, Come on, Jordy, help me. You gotta push.

I feel Bert rock beneath me, and I hear Loretta swearing. I look back, and they look scary in the weird red tail-light. I realise I have let go of the wheel. I grip it again, but I don't know if I'm gripping it in the right spot.

Loretta, I yell.

Just hold it, Tom.

But Loretta.

Bert begins to move forward. It's a quiet sound without the engine: the crunch of gravel beneath the wheels.

37

Turn the wheel, Tom, Jesus. I don't know what way to move my arms, so I just grip the wheel tighter. Bert stops moving. Loretta is at the window. She wrenches my arms to the left. There, she says.

I hold it steady, and look down into my lap. They push Bert and the car inches off the road.

Were you even pushing? she says to Jordy.

Yeah, he says.

She stalks back to the ignition and the headlights turn off. Out, she says and opens the door.

I can't see anything for a minute, so I just stand there quietly. I reach my hand out and touch the dusty side of Bert with my fingertips. He's warm and I feel okay. Loretta's face goes bright with her lighter, then there's just the orange spot of her cigarette and the smell of smoke. I see her spot of light come close to me, pass and then she's opening the boot, rustling.

It'll be alright in the morning, she says, but she's saying it to herself.

Jordy walks off into the bushes. I can see a little now, but it's a way of seeing where everything is different shades of dark and frightening. I follow Jordy out there because I don't know what else to do. I put my hand out to touch a bush, but it's spikey as pins. Jordy turns around. Stop following me, he says.

I'm not, I say. I let him walk further away. Did you hear that? I say.

What? says Jordy.

That?

What?

There are shifting shapes ahead, and the sound of breath,

movement through the bushes. I don't know whether to run towards Jordy or just turn around and run the other way. I stand there not knowing. I realise the moon is out, it hangs there like something half made.

The shapes come closer and a scream doesn't quite reach my throat. I can smell them now, of manure and dry fur. The smell of some sort of animal, but they don't have that comfort smell of hay, of grass or barn. They're all around us.

They're cows, Jordy says.

They breathe loudly. I reach my hand out to touch a flank. I can feel the startled skin beneath my fingers. The skin jumps away from me. I step back and into another warm animal. I try to stand still. The cows run. They brush against me. I close my eyes, hold my breath, make myself as small as I can. Through the sound of their hooves I can hear Loretta laughing. Her laugh is loud and sharp. I'm scared. I try to picture my dad standing with me, his hand on my shoulder. Then the cows are gone. I open my eyes and Jordy's there, close.

Did you see that? he says. So weird.

I want him to be quiet so that I can think about everything for a second. I feel maybe it's something special that all those cows were there. Like we should be quiet, and it should be cool, like when Gran makes us go to church.

I think it was special, I say to Jordy, then I want to bite my words back inside my mouth.

Special? he says. Special, like you're a retard?

He walks back to the car.

No, I say, not like that. The feeling of the church has gone. There is dust stuck to my sweat. I walk out of the dark.

Inside Bert it smells of alcohol and cigarettes. In the front Loretta has a little bottle she takes a swig from.

What's that?

It's just so that I can sleep.

But it smells.

Shhh. Enough.

She takes another swig. Jordy is silent. I try snuggle into a corner but everything I touch feels hot and horrible. I can see a triangle of the sky. It's so big and far away. It's telling me I'm nothing. I close my eyes and count to one hundred. I don't know when I fall asleep, maybe seventy-seven.

Loretta, Loretta, I say. She is curled up in a ball on the front seat. Her bare feet hanging off the edge. Loretta.

She wakes up and looks straight at me. She has creases from the pillow on her face. Her eyes look too blue.

What?

Nothing.

She puts her face back in the pillow. Fuck, she says, fuck, fuck, fuck, fuck.

Are you okay? I say.

Yes.

Loretta.

Just give me a minute, okay. It's too early, she says.

But it's already hot, I say. Her empty bottle is on the ground. She burrows into the pillow and it feels like I wait there for a long time. I see the sweat begin to bead on her skin. Jordy is crouched outside in Bert's shade. He draws lines in the dirt, then smooths them over, then draws them again.

Loretta, I say.

Okay, she says, okay.

She pushes the pillow over the seat. It plops onto the rubbish in the back. She gropes for her sunglasses with her chipped-nail-polish hands. The chips of polish are smaller now, just little spots in the centre of each nail. She finds the glasses, puts them on. She opens her door. Her bare feet on the dirt.

Hot enough? she says. Jesus.

She swings her legs back into Bert and turns the key in the ignition. He coughs into life, then out of life.

Fuck.

What's wrong? Jordy says from his side of the car.

There's nothing wrong, we're just out of petrol. I think.

Are you serious?

Don't take that tone with me, Jordy. I smile to hear Gran in her voice again, then it's gone.

Why didn't we get some before?

I thought we were going to make it.

You're so dumb, says Jordy.

You're so dumb, she says.

You're dumb.

Is this what Gran taught you? To talk back?

No, it's what you taught me, he says.

They stare at each other. I stare at them.

What are we going to do? I say.

We just got to wait, honey bunch.

My school bag is squashed up under Jordy's seat. I pull it out. The zip makes that zip sound. I see my exercise books with my name written in my careful handwriting on the front. It still looks a bit wonky and some of the letters of my name are in capital letters that shouldn't be. I wonder why I've never noticed that before. The blue lunch box is in there and when I pull it out it rattles. I open the lid and it's the smell that comes first. It's a banana that's gone black and flat. I poke it with my finger and it's like jelly. It makes me shudder. I throw my lunch box out onto the road. It looks strange out there.

What's that smell? says Loretta.

Nothing, I say.

Look, there's something coming. Look. Quick. Tom, get out there and hail them down.

Huh? I say.

Get out there on the road and hail them down.

We all get out of Bert. I imagine what we might look like to someone driving past. Jordy and me in our crumpled school uniforms, but they're so dirty that I don't reckon they look like uniforms anymore. Loretta's got clothes she changes in and out of and back into again from her suitcase in the boot. She kind of looks clean, but her hair is tangled and wild. All of us have sunburn blooming on our arms and cheeks.

She says, They'll stop for you, sweets, come on.

But why? I say.

It's better if you do it.

She taps me on the back and gives me a smile that's a present – there you go. The bulk of a truck on the horizon. It takes a while to get close. I walk out there to the middle of the road. On the white line because it feels like it's cooler with my feet on the white. I can smell my lunch box. I wave my hands at the truck. It's heading straight for me. I wave at it. I say to myself, Hello truck. Hello, hello, hello, hello, hello.

Loretta's there beside me, and she pulls me from the road by my shirt.

You crazy thing, do you want to get run over? she says.

But you said to wave it down.

I know, but I didn't say to get run over.

She leans down and kisses the top of my head and I pull away. It doesn't matter, she says.

Way past us the truck stops. Wait here, she says, I'll go talk to him. She adjusts her clothes and disappears into the heat haze.

She's taking forever, I say.

What do you want me to do about it?

I don't know. I'm bored.

He's chewing a stick. He spits bits of twig out beside him. We're both huddled in the shade of Bert, close to the dirt. I pick ants off my feet.

Jordy, do you remember from before?

Before what?

Before, when we were little. Do you remember Dad?

Who says we have the same dad?

He spits out the twig and the spit forms a perfect ball on the gravel.

I hate you, I say and get up, being sure to brush the dirt off my shorts onto him.

Well, I hate you, he says then laughs.

I start walking towards the semi-trailer. I can smell the road cooking, and wonder if I'm disappearing into the heat too. Then Jordy'll be alone and crows can pick at his bones. I look back and Bert is a yellow smudge. The truck looms tall and clear. I see

Loretta jump down from the cab. Against the truck she looks little as a girl. She swings a petrol can at the end of her arm. When she sees me she waves a little wave, like fancy meeting you here. We walk towards each other. I hear the truck start up. It drives away. She smells of petrol.

Gee, she says, I'm tired. It's so hot.

Jordy was mean to me.

Really? That's what big brothers are for, though, you know that, right?

No. He said we didn't have the same dad.

Oh. She rolls her eyes and sighs. Sweetie, that's just not true.

I look away and we walk together not talking, staring straight ahead.

But Loretta –

Tom, I'm way too hung-over for this conversation. He's just trying to get to you. Don't listen to him.

I see a kangaroo's paw by the side of the road. It doesn't have the rest of its body. It's perfect, the pads of the paw face up, like it's waiting for a high five. I want to put it on a string around my neck. Or just hold it in my hand for a moment. But Loretta's already walking away, so I leave it, and now it looks like it's waving goodbye. I trot to catch up. Loretta sighs. I can hear the petrol sloshing in the can.

What did the trucker say then?

Nothing.

But he gave us some petrol.

Yep, he sure did.

Was he fat?

Does it matter?

Do you reckon all truckers are fat?

She looks down at me and nods her head. Yeah. She shakes the can up and down. Yeah, she says.

So we can go now?

Ahuh.

I'm hot, says Jordy. He's still down in the dirt. Loretta ignores him. I look at Jordy and think that we don't look alike at all.

She unscrews the petrol cap and tries to pour a little of the petrol in, but most of it goes down the side.

Damn, says Loretta.

What? I say.

Nothing.

You need a funnel.

I know.

She pops the boot. I look in and all her clothes are out of her bag. She digs deep in there but comes up with nothing.

I was just thinking one might appear, she says. She blows up at the hair stuck to her face, but it stays there, stubborn. She goes to just keep pouring petrol down the side of the car.

Wait, I say. Do we have scissors?

She shrugs, Yeah. She points to the glove box.

I find a shiny pair, hairdressing scissors. I grab an empty bottle from the rubbish tip in the back. They all make hollow sounds against each other. The one I got crackles when I stab and slice it all the way around. The top comes off with a raggedy edge.

Here, I say. Use this. I turn it upside down, twisting off the cap. Looks like a funnel.

Hell, who's a real man, eh? She takes it from me, pours the petrol slowly. It works.

I saw it on the telly, I say. Jordy's watching us from across the car. He gets in the front.

Done, she says.

She throws the petrol can in the boot, on top of all her clothes, and flings the funnel to the ground. Slams the boot. Jumps in the front.

Get in.

I look at the funnel. I hear Bert cough to life, smell fumes. Loretta revs him hard and whoops loudly.

Tom, come on.

I've forgotten to call shotgun again. I leave the funnel there, open the door and get in, telling myself to stop being such a pussy. It doesn't matter, it's just a bottle cut in half.

5

I wake up, and I've dribbled a large wet patch onto the pillow. Bert is parked at a rest stop with a toilet block that stands out like a baby's tooth. Loretta and Jordy aren't in the car or anywhere I can see. I throw the pillow across the seat and open the door, stumble out. My legs are asleep. I punch them, Come on, legs. I've got no idea how many days we've been driving.

Loretta, I say and hobble towards the toilets, Loretta? A semi goes past so loud it sucks my voice from the air. Loretta?

She comes out the ladies side of the block. What? What? she says. Can't I get a moment's peace?

She's changed into a dress. It's floral and floats around her as she walks. She combs her streaky hair back into a ponytail with her fingers, an elastic in her mouth, then ties it up on top of her head. She does a twirl and puts her arms out. She looks beautiful, like how I remember her from before we were at Gran and Pa's the first time, when we lived in a house and Dad still lived with us.

When we left Dad, I remember being carried to the car – a different one to Bert – late at night. I must have been much smaller because I'd never let her carry me now. When I woke up again she was standing out by the road, surrounded by sugar cane, and she was howling and crying into the night. I could hear the sugar cane hushing her, the dry stalks rubbing against each other.

After that we lived in a little apartment where you could hear someone wee in the toilet from every room. And Loretta wore her dressing gown like a second skin for what seemed like years. But before that she would always wear summer dresses with bare legs and she would sing while she did the washing-up, and she would put too much dishwashing liquid in there and slap the suds together in her hands and the bubbles would go everywhere.

What do you think? she says. But I don't say anything because I'm still thinking about everything, and how we came to be here by another road, without even the sugar cane to comfort us. She crunches on the gravel over to me. She crouches down and looks me in the eye.

Ya got pillow scars, she says and touches my cheek. Pretty tough.

Where's Jordy?

She flicks her head to the toilet block and I leave her there in the gravel to go check.

There's phone numbers and swear words written all over the

48

bricks, a mirror that's really just shiny metal and buckled. In the middle of the door there's a round hole. I look through it. Jordy is sitting in there. Framed by the hole.

Whatcha doin? I say.

What do you reckon?

A poo?

Go away, you pervert. Bloody pervy perve. Get lost.

I am not a perve.

Piss off, perve.

I'm not a perve, Jordy, I'm not.

Well, go away then, you perve.

I'm not a perve.

I get out of there. Loretta has disappeared again. I walk slowly around the back of Bert and she's down in its shadow. I get down there with her and it's much cooler. We wait for ages for Jordy. We wait so long I need to do a wee and I go and piss in a crack right down into the centre of the earth.

When he comes out Loretta asks him, Mission accomplished? Like we're all on this journey into outer space to fight aliens, and Jordy gives her a look, looks away.

Mission aborted, huh, she says.

We know we're coming to a proper town 'cos the radio works again. Loretta flicks it on and searches until she finds a song she likes – and sings it. Bert's antenna is a coat hanger in the wonky shape of a heart.

I love driving, she says and winds her window all the way down, sticks her hand out, catches the wind in her palm. She's singing and she goes to Jordy, Do you know this one?

He shakes his head. Come on, sing with me, she says

and starts dancing in her seat. Sing it.

No, he says and I start to laugh.

She sings and her voice is sweet and clear. Her hair is blowing everywhere. Dancing.

I see Jordy has to look away 'cos he can't stop a smile creeping to the corners of his lips but Loretta's seen. She smiles too. You know, I've been singing in a band.

Really? When? I say. I lean right over the seat to have a proper look at her – like she could be different with this new information. What did you sing?

Oh, you know, songs. She sticks her tongue out at me.

I laugh. No, really?

Rock and roll, guitars and stuff.

Did you play guitar?

Nup, I just sang.

Can you sing one of the songs?

No, she squeals and giggles. Too embarrassing.

Please.

No, absolutely not.

Please.

No. I'll sing this one, though. She leans and turns the radio up. Her skin looks golden in the sun. She sings really loud. I look at Jordy and when he sees me looking he starts to laugh. I laugh then and I can't stop. I laugh until it hurts and she's still singing but softer now, under her breath.

There is a town and we drive straight up its guts. It has a McDonald's but Loretta won't stop.

We're getting closer, she says. It'll ruin everything if we stop now.

And that town is gone as quick as it came. There is dirt and paddocks, but there're trees now, even though it's still dry. Then without warning things change and it's greener and there are birds.

There're signs towards a city but Loretta doesn't follow them. We skirt around the city, and for a while there are houses close together, made of bricks, with letterboxes. What's weird is that they seem strange, when they're the most normal things.

Oh my god, Loretta says.

What? I say, and look around for what's getting us. But nothing is getting us, she's excited, not frightened. Then I see it, an ocean that's a whole new one from Gran and Pa's ocean.

She stops the car and I fling forward. My stomach jumps. The seatbelt catches me, choking hard against my neck.

The ocean, she squeals.

I adjust the seatbelt and start to laugh because I can't help it. She drives into a carpark that's right on the beach. The salt in the air smells nice.

Holy shit, look at that, she says. She jumps out of the car giggling and leans over the wooden railing. The wind blows her dress up. Come on. Let's go for a swim. Do you wanna? She turns back to look at us and a couple with a dog walk past. The man leans down and whispers something in the woman's ear and she looks at Loretta and laughs. Jordy shrinks down in his seat. The man links his hand with the woman's. Their dog pulls them forward by the lead.

We don't have any swimmers, I say from inside the car.

Don't be silly, that doesn't matter, you can swim in your shorts. I get out of the car to stop her yelling across the carpark.

But they're my school shorts.

So? I'll go in my underwear, fair's fair. She's already walking down to the beach, slipping off her shoes at the soft sand and leaving her clothes in a little pile at the seaweed line.

Jordy gets out of the car.

It's hot, he says and walks onto the beach, ducking under the railing.

Yeah, I say. I follow him. I pull my shirt off and it feels like I've been skinned. Our three pairs of shoes are together on the sand. Jordy's and my school shoes look bulky as blocks.

Loretta walks into the surf, she looks back at us, and the wind blows her hair in front of her face. She's wearing baggy undies and a bra that looks grey. Her feet are in the water. Come on, she yells, it's beautiful.

Jordy laughs with the sun in his eyes. We walk to the edge. There's seaweed that's like beads on a plastic necklace. I notice a new tattoo at the small of Loretta's back. Jordy walks into the waves and dives under the first one that comes. Loretta's still near the edge jumping over each little wave and gasping as she gets deeper, the waves taking her breath away. The water is cool and foamy over my feet. I look back and check on our stuff, and I can see the nose of Bert from here.

Come on. We'll dive under the next one, alright, she says to me. When she grabs my hand hers is wet. She pulls me in. It's deeper for me. A wave comes, and she jumps over it.

The next one, she says laughing. The next one comes.

No, the next one. This one for sure, okay? Ready? She holds my hand tight and we dive under together. In the cold I can still feel the warmth of her hand in mine. I keep my eyes closed tight. There is a safe place where the wave isn't even touching us. It's silent and the moment seems to last forever. She pulls me up and I take a breath. I wipe my eyes and look at her. Her hair is dark and slicked and her eyes look too big. There's shiny teeth in her grin.

How about that, she says. The next wave slaps us both in the chest.

She sits on her dress, still in her undies, on the sand. She lights a cigarette and takes a deep drag. Jordy's down by the water.

This is the life, eh. She ruffles my hair.

What's this mean, I say and touch the new tattoo. She jumps.

Nothing.

But it's new.

Yeah.

But why'd you get it? She looks down at me, but her face is silhouetted black by the sun.

Sometimes things only make sense while you're doing them. Afterwards, it's a mystery.

Jordy walks up. She puts her butt out in the sand. Come on, let's get a wriggle on. She gets up, shakes her dress and sand goes all over me. I pick her butt up and put it in my pocket. Brush the sand off me.

Goody-two-shoes, he says to me.

What?

The butt.

I finger it in my pocket. It could be anything.

What butt? I say.

He chokes out a laugh. I smile.

I walk up the beach and the sand is deep and difficult. I see Loretta slip her dress back on. Her arms and head popping out so it looks like she's being born again.

I pick up my shirt and shoes and climb back under the rail.

Feels good, hey, she says and stretches her arms up in the air.

Uhuh, I say.

Jordy's still down there on the sand.

Loretta calls him. Jordy. Jordy.

He looks up at us but doesn't come.

Jordy, she yells. Her voice doesn't echo, it just floats on out to sea.

My shorts are stiff with salt. I pick at them. I look at my bare feet. The supermarket floor feels cool. They are red and blistered from wearing my school shoes since forever. After the beach I just pushed my shoes deep under the seat. There's still sand on my feet. I rub them together, try get it off. There's a shelf with tons of thongs, all different sizes, double pluggers with white where the foot goes. I check there's no one looking and pick my size, snap the plastic strap that's holding the pair together and put them on my feet. I go find Loretta, scrunching my toes and feeling like the flicking sound of my thongs is echoing through the whole shop, loud. Loretta's hair has gone ropey from the sea and there's a ghost of white salt on her skin. Jordy's with her. Where'd you get them?

I shrug and grin. Nowhere.

He's still wearing his shoes. He stalks off up the aisles.

What do you reckon, says Loretta, we got everything?

I dunno, I say. She's got a basket hooked on her arm. She

heads to the checkout and I follow close behind. She turns back around and slips three Caramello Koalas into her pocket. When Jordy comes back, he's wearing thongs.

Copycat, I say quietly.

Shut up.

I push past Loretta and the lady in front. The lady looks down at me.

Sorry, I say.

I go and sit on Bert's bumper out the front. I look at my thongs. Loretta comes out and throws me a koala.

Cheer up, she says. Opens the boot. I watch her take other things out of her pockets: batteries, nut bars, razors. My koala is half melted. I start with the head and suck all the caramel out until he's empty inside. Jordy and Loretta get in the car. I slide off the front and get in the back.

Loretta drives down the road that hugs the beach – with a park on the beach side and shops on the other. The breeze blowing off the ocean is cooler and the sun looks ready to give it up. I don't want to put my school shirt back on so I wind the window up. Attached to each light pole is a faded Christmas cut-out with enormous ropes of tinsel strung between. At one end of the park a stage is set up and I can see kids wearing red and white Santa hats.

How about this? she says. She drives into a carpark. We got a huge packet of hot chips in the front. Loretta gets it in her lap.

Look, she says. I'll show you a trick. If you just unfold this little bit of paper at the top, look, perfect. She puts her hand in and pulls out a fat chip. The car fills with the smell of vinegar and hot oil.

I can't reach from here, I say.

Well, you got to come closer, she says. She holds the packet between the two front seats and her and Jordy get their hands in there. I lean over and grab a handful and it's like I got golden fingers.

But I didn't see how you unfolded it, I say with a mouthful of chip.

I'll show you next time, she says.

Is there any sauce?

For sure, she says. She gets the little plastic sauce thing and snaps it open. It sprays onto Jordy's hand as he's reaching in for a chip.

Loretta, he says.

I go to dip my chip on his arm.

Get lost, he says and wipes the sauce off with an old scrunched up napkin he gets from the floor and chucks back there.

I crunch a chip in my mouth and feel it turn to mush. I chew and swallow. I reach in for another and they're going soft and sweaty in the paper. Through the window I can see kids standing up on the stage in the hats. Their mouths are wide-open, singing. They're each holding a cup with a candle in it. None of the candles are lit – it's not dark yet. It's that bright blue before dark comes. The wind is blowing in so strong the voices of them kids are blown away and I can only catch a word or two coming clear and bright as if from nowhere.

What do you reckon they're singing? says Loretta.

How am I supposed to know, says Jordy.

Somebody's a grumpy bum.

We was supposed to have our concert, I say.

Huh? says Loretta.

I was gunna sing 'Rudolph the Red-Nosed Reindeer' and Jordy had to sing 'Silent Night'.

Really? says Loretta.

Yeah, I say and look at them kids up there in their Santa hats.

We sit in Bert looking out. As it gets darker the candles are lit one by one. Faces turn bright and beautiful in the wavery candlelight. There are people clumped up against the stage now and streaming towards it. I look out my window and there is a lady and a man right there, squeezing past. The man has folding chairs in his hands and it's a puzzle to get them through the small space. I look up at them, and the lady looks down. She's old, she looks like Gran. I gasp – they've found us so quick. I open the door to try and get out but it slams into her legs.

She lets out a little scream and pulls her handbag tight under her arm. And it's not Gran at all. It doesn't even look like her one bit.

Sorry, I say. I slam the door shut.

Tom, Loretta turns around and hisses at me. What are you doing?

Nothing.

Don't bring attention.

I'm not.

We watch the old couple walk away. The man still grappling with the chairs, the lady hanging on to his other arm as if for safety.

Why does it matter, anyway? says Jordy.

It doesn't, she says.

The wind blows us the music and for a moment we hear 'Silent Night', loud like the kids was right here with us.

We'll stay somewhere nice tonight, she says, by the beach. I can't see in the dark, but I feel her give us a tight smile. Then she starts Bert and reverses out.

She goes to drive out of town, but then slows down, does a u-turn and heads back. She doesn't go to the beach, but to the main street that's quiet except for a pub at each end. She stops out the front of the first.

What are you doing? says Jordy.

I'll just be a minute. Wait here, says Loretta.

You're just going to leave us?

Jordy, it's not like it's a casino. You're not going to die. I just need a moment.

She gets out of the car, closes her door. The light snaps off. She leans in Bert's window and says, Be good. Walks away. She lights up when she opens the pub door, and then she's gone.

I need to do a wee, Jordy.

What do you want me to do about it?

I need to go.

Well, do you want to follow her in?

No.

So, quit complaining then.

I look around at the street. There's no trees or bushes to quickly go in. It's wide-open, and every now and then someone slouches by. We sit there silently for a long time. Jordy drums his hands on the dashboard.

Shut up. You're making it worse.

What? With what?

That noise.

Does this make it worse?

He starts making the sound of running water, a long *shhh-hhhhhh*. Then he laughs. I can feel the pressure of the wee in my stomach that's round and taut as a drum. He starts making the running water noise again.

I'm going to piss my pants, and the whole car will stink of piss. And then you'll be sorry.

It'll be worth it.

Jordy, I whine and clench myself tight.

Geez, he says, piss in this.

He throws me an empty chip packet. It's the Twisties one from the first day.

In that?

Yes. Jesus.

Will it fit?

Why don't you find out, dipshit.

Don't look.

I'm not looking, retard.

I face the corner and undo my pants, lean over the packet. I try to breathe calmly and relax but nothing comes out. I whimper a little.

What? says Jordy.

Nothing, don't turn around.

Why would I turn around?

I let go, and the wee feels hot as it squeezes out and streams into the bag. In the silence it makes a funny noise hitting the packet. I hold the edge of it very carefully, willing it to be big enough for all the wee. I can't stop now that I have started. I wee until there's just drips. I shake them into the bag, then try to do up my pants with one hand, and hold the bag full of wee with the other, which is impossible. I just hold it, the warmth coming through the packet to my skin.

Jordy, what do I do with the bag now?

Are you serious?

I don't know what to do.

Throw it away, idiot.

I look out at the street, and there is a bin not too far away. I try scrunch the top of the bag with one hand, open the door, slip out, keep my shorts up with my other hand. I have to shuffle old man-ish. I stumble and drop the bag. It lands on the concrete with a splat and splashes wee on my feet. I step back, try to run, remember my pants aren't done up. Zip them up and run back to Bert.

What happened?

Nothing.

I wake up to Jordy tapping me on the forehead. Wake up, he says.

What? I can smell the wee on my feet.

We got to go in and get her.

But I don't want to go in there.

Jordy gets out. My eyes feel sticky. I try pick the edges open. Wake myself up. I need a drink of water. I've got desert mouth. I find my thongs under the seat. Slip them on, get out.

I look at Bert, Should we lock it? I say.

No, we don't have the key, we won't be able to get back in.

Jordy pushes open the doors of the pub, and I walk closely behind him. I reach to hang on to his shirt, but my hand is in midair when I see Loretta. She is dancing alone in the middle of the room. She has her eyes closed and her arms out to balance herself. The dress was pretty this morning. But it looks wrong in here, too short and the strap keeps falling off one shoulder. She shrugs it back up as part of her dance. She is mouthing the words to the song. There is no dance floor, just space between the tables and a jukebox in the corner. The light from the pool table gives the room a green tinge. A line of men leans up against the bar. I get a feeling that's nothing I have ever felt. My face reddens and I guess this must be shame, or something there isn't a name for.

Mum, Jordy says. She doesn't pause in her dance, her dress floating around her legs. He says it again, Mum. The men are looking at us now, all in their line. One of them nudges another who turns his face and his beer towards us. They all look a little bit the same, not like they're related, but that working the same jobs in the same sun has given them all the same hard faces. One of them adjusts his crotch, another laughs into his beer at us. If the floor opened up and inside the hole were poisonous snakes, I'd step into the hole and hope the ground closed over the top of me.

Loretta, Jordy says louder.

She opens her eyes, stops dancing. Walks over to us as if we are the only ones in the room. She puts her hands on my shoulders.

What's up? she says and then looks up at Jordy too.

I can smell the booze on her breath, but I feel better with her there close. You guys want to go?

What do you reckon? says Jordy.

Alright, she says, like it's nothing.

She stands up and twirls around. Jordy steps backwards, pulling me back with him. He doesn't open the pub door, waits for her. She stands in the middle of the room, missing something. The men at the bar holler at her but she ignores them. She walks to a table, picks up her bag and heads for the door.

You kids shouldn't be in here, one of the men yells.

I look down, make sure not to look up at them. The floor is carpet, and it's trodden down in a worn line from the door to the bar. I step away. I don't want to be standing on their dirty path.

Loretta leans over us and opens the door. Out, she says.

Nice arse, I hear called from the bar and laughter dies as the door closes. Out in the street it smells of the ocean. I inhale great big breaths. Jordy's already in the car.

I look up at Loretta and her face is real different to when we were inside. In the pub she looked serene, her face blank. Out here she looks craggy, older than she is by a million years. She stumbles as she walks, opens the front door of Bert and falls into the seat. I get in the back.

She's got a cigarette clamped between her lips and she's flicking her lighter, but it's only sparking, no flame.

Shit, she says, shit. Jordy leans over the gearstick, takes the lighter from her hand and just like that, makes a flame. She leans in.

Thanks, she says. She fiddles with the bangles on her arm. Jordy throws the lighter to the floor.

I got these for you, she says. She reaches deep within her bag and pulls out two Violet Crumbles. She throws us one each.

I got them for you, she says as if she's forgotten she's already said it. She takes a long drag of her cigarette.

We got a long way to go tonight, she says and revs Bert. Let's hit the road, Jack, she says.

I know she's drunk, but I want to leave so bad I don't care about the ad where everyone dies. We drive out of the town.

I bite through the chocolate and let my saliva melt the honeycomb. I look out at the night and a tear surprises me, just one, slipping down my cheek. I eat the chocolate bar very slowly. Loretta is driving fast. Every now and then she loses the road and drives onto gravel, but she always swerves back. I can just hear Jordy snoring in the front.

Loretta, I say.

Yes.

Are you awake?

Well, I'm driving, aren't I?

Yeah.

Well, I'm awake.

Are we going to stop soon?

I wanna find somewhere nice to stop, I haven't found anywhere nice.

It's dark.

Yeah, it is.

How will you know if it's a nice place?

We'll be able to smell the ocean again.

I open the window and all I can smell is dust.

But we've been driving for ages.

I know honey bunch, but we're on a road trip. This is what you do on a road trip. Keep talking, she says. Keep me awake.

My mind goes empty. I can't think of anything to say. Bugs splatter against the windscreen. I hear their bodies cracking open on the glass.

6

I open Bert's door when it's still early and grey. Out in the ocean there are tankers lining the horizon. They look like Lego boats. I slide down a rocky cliff. The water's got a sheen to it, a pretty rainbow. When I look back at Bert I can see Jordy standing there, looking out at me. There's a grotty boat ramp. I go look at it. It looks slippery. I climb back up the little cliff. I'm careful of shards of rock.

Where's Loretta? I say.

Jordy points to the car. Loretta's still in the driver's seat, but half in, half out, with her head hung in her hands. I go look at her. Blonde hair hanging over her face.

This is nice, I say.

She looks up, looks like she's going to get angry. But it's like she can't decide whether I'm being serious or not, so she doesn't say anything. She scrapes her hair away from her face. She leans back in the seat and closes her eyes. I go stand at the edge of the little cliff, climb back down it and collect some pebbles. I throw them into the sea. They're not flat enough to skim. They don't make much of a splash. The water just swallows them up. Jordy comes, he starts throwing rocks too. His rocks all go further than mine, but they get swallowed up just the same. We hear Bert start and I turn quickly, my heart going, but she just beeps and I see her arm waving out the window for us to hurry up and get in.

We drive through this new town. The highway goes right through the middle of it. It doesn't feel like a beachside town. It's too early for any shops to be open, but the sun is up.

They all look the same, says Jordy. Even the Christmas decorations are the same as the last town. I look up at them hanging dull and faded from the streetlights.

We're nearly there, says Loretta.

Where? says Jordy.

It's a surprise, says Loretta.

Are we really nearly there? I say.

Yep. Then she laughs, like she can't quite believe we've made it. She slaps the steering wheel. Then we still drive all day. The sun chases me across the back seat, burning one arm and then the other.

She is humming a song, every now and then singing a snatch of words, like she can't remember the rest. There's no radio reception, she's humming to the beat of her fingers on the steering wheel. There's a welcome sign to a new town. It's pock-marked with bullet holes. The light shines through it.

Can you feel it? says Loretta. She leans over and pokes Jordy in the stomach. In your belly there, can you feel that feeling?

No, stop it, says Jordy. He pushes her hand away.

She sings louder now and it's much more obvious that she doesn't know any of the words, at all. As we drive into the town, I don't feel anything.

Loretta pulls over. Wait here, she says back at us as she goes into a store. Each of the shops has Christmas greetings and decorations painted on the glass. They look like they've all been painted by the same person. Some are just holly, or Happy New Year, or Merry Christmas. This town has got a beach too, but it's like the town's ignoring the sea, turning its back towards it.

I open Bert and step out into the sun. It's still hot, but a different type of afternoon bright. My legs wobble. My shirt is damp with sweat. I wipe my face on my sleeve.

Loretta walks back out through those flappy, coloured fly strips. She looks beautiful again. She smiles at me and I can't help but smile back. She gets back in the front.

In ya pop, she says. And I get back in.

Here, she says and throws a giant bottle of lemonade back at me. I squeal with the cold of it on my legs. Jordy sniggers. I hold it between my knees and open the top. Lemonade spurts everywhere. I close the lid quick. It dribbles down the sides of the bottle onto my legs.

Loretta looks back at me. I look out the window. A rusted white truck drives past. The street is empty again. Loretta pulls the bottle from me, and opens it hanging her arms out the car window. She waits until it stops foaming before passing it in to Jordy.

The lemonade dries and sticks my legs together and to the

seat. Then dirt sticks to the lemonade. I try and shuffle out of the lemonade patch, but my skin's already sticky and there's no shuffling out of my skin. I sigh.

Can I have a sip? I say.

Jordy gives me a look, You forfeited your go, he says.

Loretta.

Give your brother a sip, Jesus, she says.

He hands me the giant bottle, letting go too soon so I almost drop it. I take a huge swig. It's cold and bubbly down my throat. I feel it try to bubble up my nose.

Can I've a sip? Loretta says to me. I pass it back to her with a grin. See, she says, we're almost there.

We cross a big bridge that looks like it's made for flood, but there's no water at all, just the silky sand of the riverbed exposed for anyone to have a look. I see the glitter of smashed beer bottles down there. We pass empty paddocks and a big roadhouse. We keep driving. There's a turnoff to a gravel road with a faded sign. Loretta passes it, then brakes hard, pulls onto the side of the road. Bert hums and ticks.

This is it, I reckon, and gives us a wink, but I can hear a tremble in her voice.

Really? says Jordy, quietly, looking out the window.

We have to be quick, the light's going, she says and does a u-turn. Drives back to the sign and turns onto the gravel road.

Out the window is red dirt and low silvery bushes. Here there are no real trees. We race the sun to the horizon. Everything rattles on the corrugated road. The back end of Bert swings out and Loretta has to spin the wheel hard back the other way.

Loretta, I feel sick, I say.

A kangaroo bounds out of the scrub. It stops and stands on the road. We are driving straight for it. I think it looks me in the eye. It's as big as a man. I can see the muscles under kangaroo skin. Loretta brakes and my seatbelt catches me. Somehow Bert spins right the way around and we're left facing the way we came, half off the road. I turn around and look out the back window. I see the kangaroo bound away through the dust. I can see kangaroos everywhere now, their heads taller than the scrub. The wind blows fumes from the car back at us.

Loretta is laughing maniacally, then she stops. If we hit one, she says, one of you has to go check its pouch.

What? says Jordy. No way.

One of you has got to, she says and squares me in her gaze. I can't do it, she says.

I don't want to, I say.

Do you wanna save a life?

Yes.

Well, you gotta check its pouch.

Why can't you do it? says Jordy.

I can't do it. You two are the men. You got to do it. She lifts her hand from the wheel and tucks her hair behind her ears.

Jordy pops the door open and tries to step out onto the road. The seatbelt pulls him back. He grabs for the buckle and unclicks it. His hand is shaking.

We didn't hit that one, Jordy, he got away, I say.

He just sits there on the edge of the seat with his feet outside the car. Leaning out of my window I see his feet placed neatly in a corrugation, his hands are crossed over his knees and his too-long hair covers his face.

Jordy, I say, Jordy – real quiet like, so Loretta can't hear.

I'm tired, I say. I wanna get there. I lean and tap him on the shoulder. He swings his legs back into the car and slams the door shut.

Loretta reverses and swings the car around, turning the steering wheel with her bony elbows in the air until we're facing the right way again. With the last light shining right at us I can see fine hair on Loretta's face. It's lit up and golden.

Go slower, I say, or we'll hit one.

I hang out the window of the car and watch the road get swallowed. There are so many kangaroos. Loretta drives slow for a while, but gets faster and faster until we're swerving all over the road again. Under my breath I'm saying, Please don't hit one, please don't hit one, please don't hit one, please don't hit one, please don't hit one. All the kangaroos turn their heads to look.

The ocean appears, the sun dipping into it. We're high up on top of red cliffs. Loretta slows down heaps and I see a huge kangaroo with its chest puffed right out scratching its belly at us. Stay there, I say to it as the road turns along the edge of the cliff. Below us there is a bay and a beach with tents at one end, then caravans. From up above, the tents and caravans look like rubbish washed in with the tide. Further than that is the white lick of a dry river. A jetty sticks into the sea. Loretta accelerates and I lose my stomach as we drive down to the beach.

The road levels out again, and goes right through the middle of the tents. They are set up along the dunes, next to the beach, four-wheel drives nudged in beside them and there are tents on the desert side of the road too. A little boy with a round face waves at us as we pass. His whole family is there, out the front of a giant tent. For a second, I can see all the way into the tent, with each of their beds made up neatly, neater than a bedroom. Some camps have their lanterns on already, casting circles of warm light swarming with bugs. There are people sitting in folding chairs, sipping wine out of plastic cups, or beer out of cans. The smell of sausages cooking. I can hear kids playing, it's the sounds of screaming and laughing together. Guy ropes criss-crossing each other with towels and clothes hanging from them so they look like banners or flags.

Why is everyone staring at us? says Jordy.

They're not, says Loretta.

Yes, they are.

It's just because we're new.

So they are staring at us? he says.

Yeah, 'cos we're new.

I'm staring at them, I say.

All the people look golden in the last afternoon light. As we drive further along the road the tents stop. There are caravans then. They've got iron sheds built around them and television antennas sticking way up high into the air, trying to catch something. They're all rusted and falling down and look like they've been here forever, like they've grown from the ground and then died of thirst. Husks of them.

Some of the caravans are nestled in the dunes, with space between each one. Further down there are two caravans facing away from each other as if they've had an argument. And here I can't see any people. They look lived in, though. There are towels hanging on washing lines, and light at the windows. But they're closed off to the road, not like the tents with their doors like open mouths and everyone sitting outside in the open. Between each caravan I can see the beach and the choppy ocean.

70

Loretta stops beside a rusty white caravan with a blue stripe. It's tucked in right behind the dune.

This it? she says and answers herself, Yep.

A cloud of dust floats from behind us and settles on Bert. None of us make any move to get out of the car.

Well, here we go, Loretta says and all three of us get out. Empty bottles tumble out around my feet. The air smells of seaweed and barbeque. I can still hear the tent kids squealing but I can't see them. I stick close to Loretta, and when she stops at the door of the caravan I bump into her.

Hey, she says, jangling her keys in her hand.

This caravan doesn't look lived in like the others do. There are thick cobwebs around the windows and doorframe, and beach grass has grown up around the step. The lock and handle are rusty. Loretta searches through the keys on her key ring, finds the one she's looking for and tries it in the lock.

You have a key? Jordy says.

Yeah, says Loretta.

How do you have a key?

What does it matter, sweetie. I swiped it from Gran ages ago. They don't come here anymore.

Loretta jiggles the key but the door stays shut. She jiggles it again and the handle makes a horrible scraping sound. Jordy and I are standing right behind her.

Shoo, she says, just shoo for a second. I look at Bert and three of his doors are wide-open. Loretta steps back, lights a cigarette and blows smoke at the door, with her back to us.

An old man walks up from a path through the dunes to the beach. He has a big fish on his fingertips and a bucket in his other hand. He smells of rotten guts. He stops when he sees us there. He has wiry arms with old-man skin hanging off them.

Who are you? he says. I see Loretta jump and she turns, her cigarette burning close to her hand.

Nobody. Who are you? she says, not waiting for the answer. She turns her back on him with a flick of her hair. She bumps her shoulder on the door to open it. It makes the worst kind of noise. I see a flap of lino scraping up behind the door. She turns back to us. Triumph makes her face shine.

He says, You got water?

No, says Loretta.

You need water – there ain't no water out here.

He shakes his head at us and walks to the caravan opposite. He goes around the side of it. When he comes back he has swapped the dead fish for a two-litre container of water, which he dumps in front of Loretta.

You're going to have to drive back out in the morning and get water from the roadhouse. Then he says over the top of Jordy's and my heads, I don't like kids. Best if they stay away.

I stare up at him – he's tall and skinny as a straw. His eyes are watery blue and fearful. I look at Jordy. The breeze blows his fringe away from his face and for a second he looks like someone else again. When I look back at the old man he's looking at Jordy too. Jordy wraps his arms around himself. The old man shakes his head, shaking a thought, and turns his back on us.

O-kay, thanks, see ya, says Loretta and rolls her eyes. I find myself waving to his back – even though he's only walking to the other side of the road. Stoopid old coot, she says and steps into the dark caravan. The sun has gone. The old man must light a lantern 'cos his windows are bright and I see him in there, his white face through the rounded windows of his caravan. He's looking out at us.

Come give me a hand, Loretta says from the dark. Jordy clumps in, banging on the metal step. I feel salt on my skin. The wind is cool. It tugs at my shirt. I go back to Bert and close two of his doors, sit half in him with my legs hanging out.

Rudolph the red-nosed reindeer had a very shiny nose – like a light bulb, I sing quietly under my breath, mumbling the words I can't remember.

Loretta sticks her head out of the caravan. Tom, she says, don't you wanna come in?

I scrunch my hands into Bert's seats. Yeah, I say.

Well, come on, she says and smiles really big.

I close Bert's door and it slams accidentally. Sorry, I hiss at him and walk away.

I pull on the caravan screen door. The step is tinny under my feet. My eyes adjust to the darkness inside. Loretta and Jordy are sitting at a tiny table with a candle between them. The candle wavers. Loretta scrapes the water bottle across the sandy tabletop and it makes my skin crawl.

Well, that looks like a bed, says Loretta. I can see one end of the caravan taken up by the square of a mattress. And I reckon you two could sleep here, she says and pats the seat she's sitting on.

What about sheets? I say.

We'll find them in the mornin', sport.

She gets up and starts opening cupboards one by one, looking inside them. She leaves them all open.

Here we go, she says. She gets three cans out of the cupboard, and dumps them on the table. One of them has no label, on the

73

other ones the labels are faded and disintegrating.

That one's a surprise, she laughs.

She opens a drawer. The cutlery rattles. She gets out three spoons and a can opener. She sits back down and opens each can.

Sweet, she says, creamed corn, and laughs again.

I'm not hungry, says Jordy.

More for us, she smiles at me.

I rub my feet under the table. She flicks a spoon at me and it slides on the gritty sand.

I get up and close each of the cupboards, clicking them back into place. Loretta rolls her eyes. I sit back down and she dumps the can in front of me.

You little weirdo, says Loretta and she reaches over the table to ruffle my hair. I swoop from under her hand. Go on, she says. —

The corn is swimming in a milky liquid. I stir it with my spoon and try to get a spoonful that's got less liquid. It drips all over the tabletop. The corn kernels burst in my mouth. They're sweet, but I gag.

I can hear us all breathing.

I can't sleep, I say.

Shut up, says Jordy.

There are strange shadows on the ceiling of the caravan. I feel under the table and there's gum there. Jordy's feet hang out over the edge. Gran read me books before bed. They were all girl's books. Jordy always hid his head under the covers so he didn't have to listen.

I can hear the ocean whisper and growl. *Grrrrrrr, shhhhhh,*

74

grrrrrrr, shhhhhhhhh, grrrrrrr, shhhhhhhhh, grrrrrrrrrrrrrrrrrr, *shhhhhhh.* All night it growls at me. I'm terrified a wave's going to come right up and wash us away.

7

She's flung out on the mattress like a splattered bug on the windscreen. I creep up and take a good look at her feet. They aren't cracked like Gran's feet. They're smooth and small as mine.

She opens her eyes and I step back, heart racing at being caught.

I think it's Christmas, Loretta, I say.

She curls over on her side and puts her head under the pillow mumbling something. The pillow has no cover on it, and it's marked with brown stains.

I bump against Jordy's feet trying to get past, and even though he looks like he's asleep he kicks me before pulling his legs up into a ball. There's thick dust on everything, and the windows are so caked with salt I can't see through them. The caravan has a force field of salt in the exact shape of a caravan.

A blowfly is awake, battering against the window, trying for the light. I open the screen door and a whole lot of other little flies get in. They aim for my face, stick to my sweat. I step outside just in my school shorts, and the screen door screeches closed behind me.

A girl rides past on a shiny new bicycle, streamers flying from the handlebars. She stares at me like I can't see her looking. I glance down at my chest and it's pale, I have a tan only on my arms, with a sharp line where my shirtsleeves hang. It's as if I'm still wearing the shirt.

Merry Christmas, she says.

I look away, mumble Hi into my pale chest. She pedals away towards the tents. When I look up the old man is there watching me from beneath the awning of his caravan. He sees me seeing him. His legs are knobbly sticks out of his shorts. He walks around the side like he's remembered something he has to do. I go back inside our caravan and put my shirt on. Loretta and Jordy are still curled in their balls. I take a long swig of water and go back outside, saying loudly, It's Christmas. Slam the door shut.

I walk around the back of the caravan to where there is a path to the beach. Beside the path is a rusted, corrugated iron shed and inside there's a drop toilet with an old paint tin beside it, full of sawdust to cover the poos. I do a long wee down into the drop. Sprinkle some sawdust in there. Outside the toilet I follow the path to the top of the dune. It only takes a second to reach the top.

The bay is shaped in a long curl, like a hook. The river mouth breaks the beach in two. Near the river there's a jetty. I run down the dune, letting out a little whoop, and then look around to make sure no one has seen me. Laugh at myself. There's ghost crabs at my feet. Their shells are see-through. The sound of crabs scuttling into the cracks when you walk close gives me shivers, but these sand crabs are nice, they seem soft. Looking back to the caravans I can only see wonky TV aerials sticking up above the dunes. At the edge of the water I let the waves foam over my feet. I make my way across the hard sand to the jetty.

Carved into the wooden steps and railing are names, 'I was ere', and other things that read like the cryptic crossword questions that Gran used to do sitting in the dining room, calling out the questions to Pa – waiting for his answer. I run my hands over the names. Further out I look down into the water. Feel the wood, smooth under my fingertips from all the leaning. It smells of fish guts. The water swirls little fish and weeds around the pylons. Way out, off the side of the jetty, there's a big wire cage, for swimming maybe, or sharks.

The sound of an unfurling rope makes me jump. There's a man further up the jetty surrounded by small cages. Each cage at the end of a rope. He looks like a dad, like he could pick you up and swing you above his head. He's leaning over the side of the jetty lowering one of the cages into the shallows. He looks up, sees me there.

Crabs, they just walk on in there. Don't even have to do nothing. He laughs. Shakes his head. It's bloody paradise.

Yeah. It comes out of my mouth as a squeak. I brush the hair from my face and look at my feet. See the water rushing under me through the gaps in the planks. I turn quickly, walk back to the caravan. My feet burn on the hot, soft sand.

Bert is gone. I slow run, trying to stop myself from sprinting to the door of the caravan. Loretta, Loretta, Jordy, Jordy, I say.

I open the door, look in and it's empty with just the flies buzzing around. The candle is a melted stump with a black, twisted wick and there is candle wax all over the tabletop.

What? says Jordy from outside.

Nothing, I say. I jump. I try to remove the panic from my words. Where's Loretta? I say.

Loretta said to be careful out in the dunes, that when she was a kid a girl suffocated digging holes in the side of 'em. She said she'd be back in a bit, she's gone to get the water.

Uhuh, I say and step outside too, look up at the sky that's big.

This is like them shantytowns they have for abos, he says.

How would you know? I say.

From before you was born.

As if, I say. He thinks he's seen everything before I was born.

I'm gunna go check it out.

Can I come? I say, trying hard to keep the whine out of my voice.

He looks me over.

Okay, he says. But you're only allowed to talk when I say so.

Jordy walks to the centre of the road. He walks down beside the old man's caravan and I follow him. Behind the caravan there's lines of painted white rocks marking the edges of the yard. There's junk everywhere, but it's neat. Piles of things collected from the beach: planks of wood, rusted metal, driftwood that's twisted muscle. Old glass buoys hang from the back awning, dusty but like whole swirling worlds.

We step over the white rock border and into the yard, past the piles of wood. Under the awning is a little table and a chair with the memory of a bum still in it. A freezer hugs close to the caravan in the shade. Jordy lifts the lid on the freezer and looks in. I lean under his arm. Cool air makes my face tingle. Inside is a huge fish chopped into pieces. I see the frosty pink of the severed flesh. Its eye looks straight up at me – big as a fifty-cent piece.

They call a fish that big a metrey, the old man says.

Jordy drops the freezer lid onto the back of my head. I get a lungful of frozen air. Pull out of there. The old man is standing right there, close to us, as if we'd been discussing something important. I can see all the wrinkles on his face and that he's angry. Jordy turns and hisses, Run.

I run. I don't think where we're going, just follow the shape of Jordy's back. I keep him in sight and when he tires I run beside him. We both stumble and laugh. Jordy stops, puffed. I look around. We're at a cleared bit in the scrub. It's tucked into the side of a dune, and the sand is littered with pieces of hose and dirty water bottles and there's a pair of rusty scissors hanging on a stick. There's ants all around our feet. Jordy is laughing.

I've got desert mouth. I need a cordial, I say. At Gran's there was always cordial in a blue plastic jug in the fridge. I never knew what colour it was going to be inside the jug. She had three lots of cordial in the cupboard, orange, green and red – like traffic lights. She never made it strong enough, but it was always cold and a surprise. When Jordy poured it he would measure each cup of cordial with a ruler so it was exactly equal. He's taking great big breaths and my breaths are big too.

Did I say you could talk? he says.

No.

Did I say you could talk then?

No.

What about then?

I just look at him with my mouth open, full of my tongue wanting to make a word.

Okay, okay, you can talk.

I don't even want to talk to you.

Well, you're talking now.

I kick a bit of hose. It's weird here, I say.

It's alright, he says.

We can make a cubby in the dune.

Loretta said not to dig in 'em.

I imagine getting a face full of sand, and the thought of it crunching in my mouth against my teeth makes my whole body shudder. Jordy goes to a tall bit of the dune and kicks it. Kicks it again until the sand falls over his feet. I make sure to stand a good way away so that if it all collapses I'll be there to pull him out by the edge of his shirt, or his foot.

Let's go find a drink, he says.

We walk through scrub for a while before we get to the tents. I hadn't realised how far we'd run. The tents have their ropes out really far to trip us. There's a mum out the front of one and she smiles and says, Merry Christmas. I just look at her, keep walking and don't say anything back.

I think I've got sunstroke, I say to Jordy.

You have not.

I have, I feel dizzy and I'm going to vomit.

How would you even know?

They're the symptoms.

As if.

Eventually you get so thirsty you go crazy.

Whatever.

Both of us stop when our caravan comes into sight. Bert still isn't here. Just the caravan screen door banging open and shut.

Come on, says Jordy and we walk up to it. I click the screen door shut and sit on the step in the sun. Jordy looks under the caravan.

There's chairs, he says and pulls out two canvas chairs with cobwebs all over them. Jordy opens one of them and sits down in it. It looks broken but he doesn't fall. I swipe a fly from my face. He gets up. His chair buckles.

It's hot, I say.

Did I say you could talk yet? Look, an awning, he says.

He taps at a metal lever sticking out the side of the caravan, then pulls. The metal screams, and flakes of rust and dirt fall all over me.

Hey, I say. I jump up and out of there. I try shake the dirt off me. Be careful, I say.

Jordy pulls it all the way out. It's wobbly, but it stays there, and it makes a small square of shade out the front of the caravan. The edge of the canvas is black with dirt and disintegrating, but the bit that was rolled up inside the metal is brown-and-orange striped and looks new.

Cool, says Jordy. He sits back in his tumbled-down chair, righting it first so he can get in it. I sit back on the step. In the shade the rest of the world looks hotter. We sit there for a while not saying anything, then Jordy gets up.

I'm going to the beach, he says, without looking back at me. I want to follow him, but I leave it too long and then I'm just sitting there alone. I scratch a bite on my leg. I scratch it until it bleeds, then a fly lands on the wound. My stomach grumbles. I hear a car on the gravel. I see the dust before the car and I stand up, ready to run to Bert, but it's not Bert, it's an old white ute. It stops across from me, pulls up beside the old man's caravan.

He gets out of the ute and looks over at me. I don't wave at him, or say hello. He pretends he hasn't seen me. Walks to the back of the ute. He tries to lift a crate from the tray. He scrapes it along the metal and up to the side, drops it. He tries to lift it again. It falls back into the tray with a shudder. He gives up and carries the two-litre Coke bottles inside two by two, then the crate. In the caravan he would have to put them all back in the crate. I hear a generator jump to life with a loud hum.

He comes back out with a glass of Coke with ice and sits down in his chair that's sagging out the front, ready for him. He looks happy taking the first sip, but then he's staring right at me and he doesn't look happy anymore. I walk over the gravel road.

Get, he says, get out of here.

I stand just at the edge of what looks like his area and say, I'm not near you, I'm just standing over here.

Standing there's too near, little matey. I told ya, piss off.

How about here? I say and take two steps back, so I'm kind of standing in the middle of the road.

Too close, he says and takes a long sip of his drink.

I take a couple more steps back so that I'm right in the middle of the road. Here?

Too close.

I take another step back, Here?

Nup.

Until I'm right the way back under my awning and I yell, Here?

I guess that's as good as it's going to get, he says. I see him smile. I smile.

Can I've a Coke?

You want a Coke?

Yeah.

He sighs, gets up and goes inside. When he comes back outside he has a glass. I go to walk over there.

Stop.

He walks out onto the road and gives me the glass.

Thanks. I take a sip.

He walks back to the shade.

Loretta hasn't come back from getting the water.

Who's Loretta?

My mum.

What do you want me to do about it?

Nothing, I guess. I take another sip of the Coke. It's bubbly and warm. Tastes a bit like sick. I kick my feet in the dirt. We might need to go and look for her, I say.

What do you mean we?

I walk over there and cross the invisible line into his yard. There is a mean curl at the edge of his lip.

We have to go get her, I say.

He says quietly but with force, Get back over your side. And give me that. He takes the Coke from my hand. Get, he says.

I run back to our caravan and sit on the step watching him. He finishes his Coke and gets another. He rolls a cigarette, smokes it. He rolls and smokes three cigarettes with me sitting there watching him. I make patterns in the sand at the step of the caravan. The shade from the awning travels. I wipe sweat from my face and feel my bum fall asleep. He gets up, goes inside his caravan for a while and when he comes out the front again I'm still there, sitting on the step. I see him swear under his breath, turn around. When I see him next, he's got his fishing rod, a floppy hat hangs over his eyes. He walks past me, like I'm not there, and heads down the path to the beach. I brush the flies away from my face, look at the dirt between my feet. I can taste the Coke a little still. Brush the flies away again. Jordy's still gone.

The old man takes a long time to come back. It's late afternoon. My bum has moulded to the shape of the step. He sees me still sitting there. Stops in the middle of the dusty road. He doesn't look like he's caught nothing. It's just us, but he looks behind him like he's checking if there's someone else there, then he looks to the blue sky as if he's praying for rain – or something. He disappears around the side of his caravan.

I stand up, stumble. My legs don't work anymore. I run as well as I can, away from him. I run down to the beach, my feet sinking into the sand. The spinifex grass swishes in the wind I make as I pass. The sun is in my eyes and I don't see Jordy there at the bottom of the path. I run smack into him. I hit my head so hard against his elbow that I see black, and cartoon stars. We tumble down the dune together and I get sand in my pants and my mouth, ears. The beach is inside me. We're down there in the sand and I feel a sharp punch in my leg.

Get off me, he says.

I spit the sand out of my mouth. I try disentangling myself from him but he kicks my legs until we are both sitting in the sand across from each other, finally out of reach and sore. I rub sand in my eye, out of my eye.

You are so annoying, he says from across the sand.

Loretta's not back still, I say. I see him take a big breath. I think we need to go and get her, I say.

How?

We can ask the old man to drive us?

Nah.

But there's no one else. I've already asked him.

What did he say?

No.

He rolls his eyes at me and pulls his long limbs together to stand up. He shakes sand all over me. You shouldn't do stuff without asking me first.

You're not the boss.

I'm older.

Not by enough.

There's no enough. I'm still older.

I sit there in the sand as he walks away. I watch the sun and it burns my eyeballs, but I look at it just to see if I can see it falling.

At the caravan Jordy's having a drink of water. The bottle is nearly empty.

Can I've a sip? I say. He pegs the bottle at me and I drop it. The water pools in the sand, not soaking in. I stoop down to rescue the bottle and save the last mouthfuls. I try to get the sand out of my mouth, swirl the water around, but sand still crunches in between my teeth.

Be careful, he says like it was me who chucked the water in the sand.

It's going to be dark soon, I say. We stand across from each other under the awning.

Fine. Wait here, he says.

He walks across the road and knocks on the old man's door. The old man doesn't answer the door, though, he looms around the side of the caravan. I try to yell to Jordy to warn him, but it comes out of my mouth a whisper. I see Jordy jump when he notices him there in the shadows but then they're talking. The old man disappears again and when he returns he's swinging his keys in his hands, he grabs them, swings them, grabs them, swings them. The sound of the jingling carries over to me. I think of Santa's sleigh bells.

Jordy motions for me to come over and we go and stand near the ute.

Get in, Jordy says quietly, like if he said it loudly the old man would change his mind.

Jordy climbs in after me. The old man stuffs around with the radio. Can only get one station all the way out here, he says. Scraps of voices come clear, then it's fuzz. What's ya names then, eh? I look over at him and there's a drip of sweat running from his temple down the side of his face. He clicks the radio off. Damn it.

Tom, I say, and that's Jordy. Jordy's hanging his arm out the window ignoring us.

I'm Nev, he says.

I'm squashed in the middle. I try not to touch him. The ute kicks into life after a couple of rattles. I scratch gently around my sandfly bites, bite by bite. I'm careful not to break the skin again. We drive slowly on the road between the caravans. A cloud of dust hangs behind us. Nev drives out of the camp. Driving away from the falling sun, into the electric blue of the late afternoon. The corrugations rattle my teeth 'til they ache.

Did you get anything for Christmas? I say.

No. Santa stopped coming my way a long time ago.

Were you naughty?

He laughs.

I didn't get anything either.

He laughs again, but it's a different kind of laugh to the first one.

How many k's to the highway? says Jordy.

Forty.

Jordy sighs.

Nev puts the radio back on and a country song warbles out at us. Some guy with gravel in his mouth. I put my fingers in my ears.

Take them fingers out of your ears, he goes.

What? I say.

Take them fingers out of your ears. I pull them out and look up at him.

In my car you listen to this, and you app-re-ci-ate it. Alright?

I stare up at him, not knowing what to say.

Alright?

Okay, I say and he looks away first. I pick at my sandfly bites and creep up against Jordy.

Piss off, Jordy hisses and tries to push me back. You're making me hot, he says.

Nev starts tapping his hand in time. He opens his mouth and it's the smell of old man.

As we drive into the roadhouse I can see Loretta standing,

leaning against Bert. In the carpark there are bugs swarming around her, like she's the light. She's smoking a cigarette and the ground around her is covered in butts. She's staring at barrels full of water next to the tap. There's a road train parked opposite. Nev drives up to her and stops the ute. She looks at us like she's looking at strangers.

Hey, says Jordy.

Hey, she says. She grinds her half-smoked cigarette out.

Nev sighs and turns the engine off, pulls the handbrake on. Are you kidding me? What are you doing out here? he says.

Nothing.

How long have you been standing here?

I don't know, a while.

Her face looks like she's just woken up from a dream. She jiggles her leg, winds her hair around her finger how little girls do.

She says, He asked me if I wanted a hand, and I was like, nah, mate, I can lift them myself, but then I tried to lift them, and they were too heavy and then I've been waiting for him to leave so I can drag them to the car without him watching, but he's still in there, he won't leave me alone, she says all in one long breath. All around her the bugs are going crazy. It's like it's got properly dark since she started talking and now the bugs are all around the truck too. They smack into the windscreen and fly off.

Who? he says.

The guy in the truck, she says.

Are you serious?

Yeah.

From the ute I can see a dent in Bert's door in the exact

shape of Loretta's hip. I've never noticed it before.

Can I get out? I say. Jordy opens his door and jumps. I tumble out after him. The ground is further away than I remember and I fall. Jordy stands there. I go lean near Loretta and touch my hand to the back of her leg. She ruffles my hair and puts her hand under my chin to have a good look at me.

You're burnt to a crisp, she says.

Her saying that makes my face feel tight as drum skin.

I hear the ute door slam. Nev is standing there. I shrink up against Loretta's legs. He looks too tall and I get a weird vision of him in the light, what he would have looked like young, and strong, and mean. Before the wind and the sun got to him. I turn my face away.

I drove all the fucking way out here, he says. And the *guy in the truck* is probably asleep in the fucking cab.

I feel Loretta shrug. It's like he's the crazy one. She doesn't know what he's talking about, or why he's angry. She laughs. Whatever. She says it just like Jordy would.

Jesus, he says and walks off towards the roadhouse. Walking, he's old again. His wrinkly arms hang out of his blue singlet.

Loretta shrugs again and we all follow Nev. Loretta doesn't even look at the road train again. She lets the heavy roadhouse door swing shut. A man with tatts poured over his arms stares at her. She tugs her short skirt down.

Nev's at the red plastic counter waiting. A girl with long golden hair wound up in buns over her ears asks him, Can I take your order? She has an accent that makes her words round and honey but at the same time she sounds a bit retarded. She's wearing a Santa hat and flashing earrings.

Nev orders us all a meal without asking what we want.

The girl puts a number on the counter and turns away to plunge frozen chips into bubbling oil. I wonder what the girl thinks of us.

Sit down, boys, says Nev.

They're my boys, says Loretta.

Hey lady, I don't give a shit, okay.

My name's Loretta.

Through the window I can see the water barrels still out there next to the tap. There is a cow standing out by the highway. Just one lonely cow. We all sit down at a plastic tabletop shiny with grease.

Loretta pours salt onto the table and makes patterns in it with her long fingernails.

I knew a truckie, says Nev, he had his kids for the weekend, took 'em with him, and they were asleep in the cab while he was driving. He fell asleep at the wheel. When he woke up there was nothing behind him, just air. The rest of the semi and his kids were spread out across the road, but he was just sitting there perfect in the front seat like nothing had happened. Course he didn't sleep very well after that.

What's that supposed to mean? says Loretta.

I'm just sayin, he's asleep in the cab.

Loretta sweeps her salt patterns to the floor. Whatever, she says again.

It's like we're all three his children. The girl with honey in her mouth comes over with our burgers and chips. Her pale skin is red and blotchy at her cheeks and she gives us a smile that looks like it hurts. Merry Christmas, she says. Walks away.

Loretta squirts tomato sauce all over her chips and puts them in her mouth one fat, soft chip at a time. She licks her fingers and scrunches up a heap of napkins into balls. I take a bite out of my burger and burn my mouth. I spit it back out onto my plate – wait until it cools, then eat it.

So what's your story? says Loretta.

He looks her over. I ain't got a story, lady.

Oh yeah?

He leans over the table. What's *your* story then?

We're on holiday, says Loretta smiling.

He seems to lose interest, leans back in his chair and pushes his burger, half eaten, away. I eat everything on my plate, even the end bit of bread that's soggy with beetroot juice and sauce.

This is a shitty place to come for a holiday, he says from way back in his chair.

You live here, Loretta goes.

I like the quiet life. It's my sunset years. He wipes his mouth methodically with a napkin. Folds it, puts it under the edge of his plate.

I like the quiet too, she says.

Oh yeah, well, merry bloody Christmas, he says to us and gets up, goes outside to his ute.

Coming? asks Jordy. I shrug and get up. The waitress floats over. Loretta gives me a smile and scrapes her chair back and gets up too. Jordy pushes through the glass door but doesn't hold it open for me. I look back at the waitress and she's piling our plates one on top of another, but taking a long time, like she's trying to figure out the best way to do it. I push on the door, leaving a greasy handprint on the glass.

Nev is already in his ute with the engine on. Loretta lights a cigarette and we all look at him as if waiting for instructions.

You gunna get them? says Nev.

I look at the water barrels and Loretta says, Give us a hand, Jordy.

They lug them to the car and put them in the back seat. There's bags of shopping in there too. Nev revs his car.

Can you take one of the kids back? says Loretta.

No, says Nev, I'm not taking them.

I don't want you to take them, I just want you to take one of them. There's no room – can you see room? She points with a flourish to Bert stuffed with bags. You brought them all the way out here, you can take one of them back, she says.

I'm not taking them. Don't tempt me, lady.

My name is Loretta. She stands with her hands on her hips.

I'll go, says Jordy after taking a look at me. He gets up into Nev's ute. Jordy sits there staring off into the distance, but sitting as far away as he can get from Nev. I see Nev swear under his breath. But he puts the car into gear and drives off, showering Loretta and me in gravel.

Thanks, she says and I can't decide if she's being sarcastic or not. She gets in the car. The road train is still there but Loretta seems to have forgotten about it. I look up at the service station lights. The bugs swarm them. They seem big and fat enough to be shot down. They come swarm around me. Loretta honks the horn.

You coming? I get into Bert too and Loretta accelerates out of there, fast.

I look at the dark road straight ahead. Jordy is gone. I've got shotgun. I pick at the stuffing of the seat. I don't know what to say. I can't remember ever really being alone with Loretta.

When we get back to the caravan the headlights show Jordy.

He's sitting on the step alone with his arms wrapped around him. He stands up, shields his eyes against the light and walks out, blindly stepping towards us. When Loretta turns off the lights he says out of the dark, You're home? Like he didn't think we were going to be.

8

I wake up to the smell of burning. From my bed I can see Loretta at the stove. Her bony legs poking out of an enormous jumper, but it ain't really cold, just dark. She turns off the flame and catches me watching.

You're awake, she says.

I close my eyes.

I saw you, she says, I know you're awake.

She scrapes the beans onto three plates.

Wake up, Jordy, she says. Tom, I know you're awake, wake up, Jordy.

I hear him rustling, and I pretend to be asleep. Dead still. She nudges my feet and puts the plates on the table.

You hungry? she says. You hungry?

I sit up and she laughs at me. See, you are awake. She scrapes the little stool up to the table and starts spooning baked beans into her mouth. Hot, she says, and blows on them. I wonder if I'm dreaming a boring dream.

I try to open my mouth to say something, but it's stuck together. I try again. It's the middle of the night, I say.

Dinner, she says.

I rub my face hard.

Jordy, she says, dinner.

I drag the plate towards me over the sandy tabletop. The sound gets inside me and makes me squirm. When I taste the beans they're smoky with burnt.

Good, hey, says Loretta. Jordy, she says, it'll get cold, eh.

I blow around the beans in my mouth, swallow and say, Hot.

Jordy pulls the sheet over his head and turns to the wall. Loretta holds his foot in her hand, but he pulls it away. She puts that hand palm up in her lap, spooning beans with the other.

Next, we'll go north, she says. All we have to do up there is drink beer and watch out for crocs.

Seagulls scuttle on the caravan roof, fighting over something. I lick sauce from the corner of my mouth.

Are seagulls nocturnal? I ask.

Nocturnal's a big word.

But are they?

Hell, sweetie, I don't know.

I can hear them, I say.

Well, that's your answer then.

I guess so.

I worry we woke them up. And I wonder what they've got to fight about up there. I spoon more beans into my mouth.

Drips fall from my spoon to the table.

I'm full, I say. My beans still half eaten.

Okay, she says.

Should I go back to sleep?

Yeah, why not?

I lie back down on my seat but I can't sleep. After a while there's pink light at the windows. And then the light goes white. I sit up. Loretta's still at the table. She hasn't eaten much, she's mostly pushed the beans around on her plate. Jordy's plate is cold and the sauce looks hard.

Morning, she says.

Morning, I say.

I push past her, put my dirty plate in the little sink. Through the salty glass I see the girl ride past with her new bike, but it looks old. It's rusting already.

The morning's hot enough for us to be sweating pools onto the tabletop. Jordy's out front flicking flies away with his fringe, like a horse with its tail.

Loretta's got an opened-out beer carton and a Texta. She writes 'Haircuts $10'.

Here we go, she says.

The plastic of the bench farts as she gets up, and I laugh — she crinkles her nose at me and goes outside with her sign. She leans it against the side of the caravan, stands out on the gravel and admires it. Stoops back under the awning, touches Jordy's hair.

Don't, he says. Can you even cut hair?

Yeah, she puts her hands on her hips.

Your sign's on a beer carton.

I used to work in a hairdresser's.

Oh, yeah.

You don't know everything about me.

She sits down in the wobbly canvas chair to wait. I stand at the screen door letting the flies into the caravan.

Put the kettle on would you, Tommo, she says.

I turn around and fill up the kettle from the water bottle. I light the gas carefully, but still I smell burnt hair. I wait for the whistle. Just that little flame makes the caravan hot as an oven and I get out of there.

Jordy stands and walks down the little path towards the toilet, Where are you going? I say.

Nowhere, he calls back to me without looking around.

Loretta goes to me, Well, you wanna be me first customer?

Alright, I say and let a smile break out on my face.

Okay, she says, getting up. Sit down, Mr Customer.

I sit in the chair, balancing on it so it doesn't tumble.

She gets a towel from inside and tucks it around my neck.

Got to find my scissors, she says and goes and leans into Bert. She holds them up, triumphant, the silver glinting in white sunlight.

The towel is scratchy and stiff from salt. Loretta runs her fingers through my hair.

Don't know where you inherited this from, she laughs.

Gran says her dad's was like this.

Loretta scoffs, What would Gran know?

I look in my lap. My hair starts to fall around me. The snips of the scissors seem loud.

How short, Sir?

I dunno, I say.

Hmmm, well, we'll just make you look like a movie star then, huh? I can smell her, standing so close. I must smell too, but she smells so strong I want to hold my breath. Loretta goes, Lucky you ain't a girl. It's much harder to cut a girl's hair. With you, I can just measure off the horizon. She laughs. I listen to the snip, snip of the blunt scissors.

The kettle starts its whistling scream. She snips my ear and I jump out of the chair.

Ow, I say.

The chair collapses. I touch my ear and my fingers come back bloody.

Loretta, I scream at her.

Shit, she says, it's bleeding like buggery. She has the scratchy towel in her hands. She clamps the towel to my head.

I hate you, I say and pull away from her. She drops the bloody towel. The kettle still screams. I run down the path to the beach. The ghost crabs scatter. I put my feet in the water. It foams up around my ankles. I feel my ear, the scabby blood. I try not to cry. Jordy's there then, standing beside me.

What happened? he says.

Nothing, I say and hold my ear.

There's blood.

Loretta cut my ear.

He raises his eyebrows at me, Really? Laughs and says, Jesus.

I can't figure out what's strange about him. I realise he's not wearing his school shirt. He's wearing a huge white singlet that falls off his shoulders. I can see the bones in his back. I'm not wearing my shirt, it's scrunched up like a used tissue somewhere in the caravan.

99

Where'd ya get that? I say.

From Nev.

He let ya have a singlet?

Yep.

When?

He gave it to me.

That's not fair.

Jordy shrugs.

I look down at my hollow chest and figure I'm burning. My shoulders already feel too hot. A breeze blows at me and flutters my uneven hair. It's long all to one side. It settles back on my sweaty forehead.

We walk along the hard bit of wet sand. So many fishing lines stretch into the water. They're streaming like a party. Lures and pilchards catch the sun. I wonder if I stand behind a fisherman when he's flicking the line behind him, ready to swing it in a big curve into the sky and it makes that noise of the line unfurling from the reel, if the hook could catch right into my face, through my cheek. I'd be too heavy to be flung like the lure is, into the sea. I'd just be caught on the beach.

Pa used to drag an orange bag full of guts, bones and fish heads along the beach, looking for worms. They're long and they stick their heads up from the sand. He'd pull them up, thread the hook through their mouth, then push it right the way along their whole body. See the black hook through the skin.

There he is, I say. Not Pa, Nev. Down here he don't look so much like an old man. He leans his arms back and flings the line in a smooth arc out past the breakers, then starts winding it back in quick. Jordy touches my arm.

Let's – he says, but stops because Nev turns to look at us

like he can feel us standing there. We keep walking towards him. He reels in the line. Then we're close enough to smell his cigarette smell. He pulls a little puffer fish in on the end of his line. It flaps around on the wet sand.

He doesn't say hello. He says, They ain't good eating, but they ain't good for nothing.

He puts his thong over the breathing body of the fish, pushing against the poisonous spines and removes the hook from the side of its fish mouth. It gasps.

Here, he says. He passes the hook and line to me. I step forward and hold it between my fingertips. He rolls a cigarette, lights it up and looks us each in the eye. I wrap the line around my finger too tight.

He takes his foot off the puffer. When I seen puffers slip through the shallows they were little, but it's starting to puff right up on the beach. He kneels down in the sand. A wave threatens to foam over us, it wants the fish back. He sucks in deep on his ciggie, ashes it beside him then sticks the filter of the ciggie in the little fishy mouth of the puffer, between its barbed teeth. The fish puffs up with smoke. There is a spot of blood on the wet sand. It's puffing smoke right into its belly. The ash on the end of the cigarette stays whole like it does when Gran's friends forget to ash them. Little puffs of smoke escape but most of it goes inside. Its body gets huge and round, its fins sticking out like branches. I test the sharpness of the hook on my thumb and scrunch my feet into the sand.

The puffer fish loses its shape. Its beady eyes are pulling inside its skull. Nev steps back. We lean in. It bursts. It makes a popping sound. A little bit of gut gets on my knee. Shiny and slimy. There are flappy bits like burst balloon around the fish. Smoke comes out of the holes. He laughs. The butt's still gripped tight in the fish's teeth. I lean down, pick the butt from its lips and put it in my pocket. I rub the guts off my knee.

See, he says. He pulls the line from my hand and the hook scrapes against my palm.

Ow, I say.

Come on, says Jordy. He pulls my arm. Nev is still laughing, shaking his head. A gull flies down to peck at the carcass and screeches at us to get away.

Come on. I'll show you something, Jordy says. We walk away from Nev and when I look back he's not following us, he's just staring out to sea.

Further down the beach, there are tons more people. Jordy walks towards them and I follow him, stepping in his footprints in the sand. I have to jump between them because his legs are longer. When we get to the people I don't look any of them in the eye. I look at their legs standing in the sand, their thongs and brown feet. Hear the sound of fishing rods coming away from the spool, then the clicking of them being wound back in. We walk under the lines stretching into the waves. They say G'day to us, and Jordy scowls. I pick at my ear scab and it starts to bleed again. I put spit on it to try make it stop and the blood on my fingers tastes like metal. In the wet sand I can see the patterns the little snails make. I follow Jordy up into the hot sand, the dunes shrugged up around us, then back onto the gravel road. There are tents everywhere. Kids screaming and running. The drone of cricket announcers from a radio somewhere. We walk past the tents. All their awnings opening towards the road. We walk until the tents get sparse. The road becomes skinnier and then Jordy walks into the scrub that the tents turn their backs to. We walk until the point where the white sand around the camp turns to red and loop back around so we're headed towards the back of the camp.

I'm hot, Jordy, I say.

Don't be a pussy.

My shoulders are burning.

I see it. It's just standing. Jordy's magicked it there. A kangaroo as pale as white sand. Jordy whistles between his teeth and it cocks its head at us.

Is that what you wanted to show me? I whisper.

No.

We creep past it and it stares at us the whole way. When I look back, it's gone and I can't even picture where it was standing.

Do you reckon you could have a kangaroo as a pet?

No way.

Why not?

What do you reckon?

I don't know.

They'd go bad. You couldn't ever tame them properly.

Really?

Really.

You think you know everything.

Do not.

Do so. I hear him take a huge breath and sigh.

Remind me why I let you come? But I can tell it's a joke.

You asked me to come.

Whatever.

From here we can see the backs of the tents. The bushes scratch at my bare legs. Jordy nudges me and we walk closer towards them.

Be quiet, he says.

I am quiet.

Shhh.

You're the one talking.

He punches me hard in the shoulder. Corks me bad, and I have to gulp in breath to stop myself crying out.

He whispers, Look, but I've got no idea what he's talking about. Go get us some beer.

What? I say. I see a huge esky now, beside the tent. No.

Don't be a pussy, pussy.

I don't want to, Jordy, I say. We're so close I can smell him, different to Loretta, and coming from his singlet is the smell of laundry powder. It reminds me of at Gran's how our clean clothes would always be in a neat pile at the end of our beds, warm from the iron and smelling of fresh.

Come on, don't be a pussy.

I'm not being a pussy.

Yeah, you are.

Shut up.

Useless, he says and shuffles towards the tent. I shuffle backwards. It's a huge triangle tent with crossbars at the back and front. I can hear people in it. I see Jordy at the esky and I hear the plastic creak of the lid opening as loud as if it was right beside me. He pulls out a bright six-pack of cans – held together with those plastic things that get around penguins' necks and they starve to death 'cos fish can't fit down their throat.

He grins at me. He rests the beers in the dirt for a moment, pulls a shirt off the guy-rope – there's washing pegged along it. Grabs the beers again and runs.

Here, he says and throws the shirt at me. It's warm. Come

on, he hisses and runs back into the red sand. Beside me is a flower, bright as fresh-spilt blood. I run after him.

We sit on the sand so far along the beach the tourists are anty. Jordy cracks one of the beer cans and it foams over his hand. He gives it to me, and I'm so thirsty I skol it. It's luke warm and horrible in my mouth. He cracks one for himself and leans back on his elbow as he gulps it down.

Do you miss Gran? I say.

No, he says.

Would you rather be with her or Loretta?

He scoffs at me. What do you reckon? he says, but I feel wrong inside because I don't know what I reckon.

I finger the sleeve of my new T-shirt. It has Winnie the Pooh on it. I put it on inside out so that Pooh is facing to my chest. I like him in there. Jordy skols the beer and gets up, throws his too-big singlet to the sand, and slips out of his shoes.

I'm goin' for a swim, he says. He pegs his can at me. Beer pools out.

The ocean is shiny, blue and much rougher here than at the curl of the bay where the caravans are. The dumpers dig at the beach. Jordy times the waves, dives. He swims straight out until he's through all the breakers and I can only see the dark spot of his head.

I get up to follow him but I'm so dizzy I have to lean down and steady myself halfway. I pick up a shell. There's mostly just flat ones with oil slick insides, and little tiny snail shells. I see the edge of one, half in the sand, lean down, dig it out, tap the sand out of it. It's a white shell as long as my palm. The snail's body inside it would be the shape of a spiral, going right up into the tip. I look up. Jordy's way out in the ocean. I stand up slowly. I put the shells in my pockets. I feel the jumble of sandy shells in there.

I walk to the edge of the waves, so that I can keep his head in sight. I imagine what I'd do if I saw him get eaten by a shark. I'd see the fin, and then thrashing, and then blood in the water. A headache booms out at me from nowhere.

Come in, I whisper to myself, come in, come in, come in. I dig my feet deep into the cool sand and wait. A seagull swoops down to check me out, then catches the breeze back up into the sky. Come in, come in, come in, come in. The pain in my head keeps time.

Where've you been? says Loretta.

At the beach, says Jordy and bangs the screen door shut behind him. It's hot under the awning and the beer carton hairdresser sign has blown over.

You have to tell me where you're going. How am I supposed to know where you are? she says to Jordy's back. And where'd you get that shirt? she turns to me.

Nowhere, I say. Still standing in the sun. I inch into the shade.

Don't lie to me, Mister.

Jordy gave it to me, I say. I'm not lying.

Don't talk to that old man, he's a drunken weirdo, okay? She comes and holds my face in her hands. You're burnt to a crisp, she says, again.

Her hair looks like a windsock in the hot northerly.

Okay, I say. Have you had any customers?

Don't be a smart-arse.

I wasn't. I was just asking.

I pull my face away and go into the caravan. Jordy's in there, sitting up at the table. I can see the fan of sweat across his cheeks and nose. He's got a plastic cup full of water. I get my own cup and pour from the container. Wipe my face on my sleeve.

How's your ear? Loretta yells from outside.

Fine, I say quietly.

What?

Fine.

Jordy sniggers at me. His singlet slips off his shoulder and he shrugs it back up. I take the shells out of my pockets one by one, line them up on the table. Sometimes it feels like having a mean older sister.

The night is at that bit where it's not black yet. It's the darkest blue. Loretta opens a can of spaghetti and pours half each on a plate for Jordy and me. The plates here are plastic and so cut from knives and forks that the plastic has gone furry. The other plates are still dirty in the sink.

Aren't you having any? I say.

Nah, she says.

It's cold, I say.

She shrugs, steps back down the step of the caravan and we go out too. I'm careful not to tip my plate of red and worms. She lights a cigarette, leaning over, like she's going to burn her hair. I fork the spaghetti into my mouth and mosquitoes bite me. Every couple of minutes is the sound of us slapping them.

Jesus, says Loretta and goes back into the caravan. I can hear her rustling around in there. She comes back out shaking an old aerosol can. The rattle of it. She leans over me and sprays my legs and arms.

Owww, I yell. That kills.

What, she says, what?

It kills.

The spray is right in my scratched sandfly bites.

Jordy looks at us both and says, No thanks.

Suit yourself, she says, and with her ciggie clamped in her lips she sprays her own legs and arms and attempts to spray her back. She sits in her chair, stubs out her cigarette, half smoked, and lights another. I scrape the last of the spaghetti and wipe the plate with my finger until it's clean. It tastes of Aerogard.

Let's do something fun then, eh.

I look to Jordy but he's looking across to Nev's caravan. The windows are bright, but I can't see Nev in there.

Don't be so excited, she says.

What do you mean? I say. The spaghetti is heavy in my belly.

We're going to go floundering. Did Pa ever take you floundering?

No, says Jordy.

I'll teach you. It's perfect for it here. Last time we caught millions of fish, a million years ago. You could still smell them for days after we fried them.

You caught them? Jordy says.

Yeah, I totally caught them.

Here?

Yes. Come on, we'll be eating the secret side of a flounder soon as. She gets up, flinging her butt to the sand where it glows before fading out. We need gear, she says and goes looking in the caravan again.

I sniff in a deep breath and see if I can smell the lingering fishy smell. I hear banging from inside. She comes out with some rope, a torch and a small blunt-looking knife.

We got to get a stick from somewhere, sharpen it, she says. I can smell fish. But it's the smell of rotten scales and guts. The screen door bangs shut behind her as she steps down.

Come on, it's going to be great, she says.

I look back over at Nev's caravan again, he's not inside in the light, he's in the dark next to it, leaning on the side looking out. He's black except for the orange bum of his cigarette that brightens his face with each suck in. I look in my lap and count to ten hoping he's gone by the time I look up again.

Loretta's striding out front with the torch. She leaves us to walk in the dark. There's lantern light at some tents, pools of it. Some glow from the inside and I can hear low murmuring. From everywhere there's the sound of people slapping mozzies. Most tents are dark, though. The stars are low and bright. I can hear the slap, slap of her thongs. She stops.

Look for sticks, she says. I look around but there are no trees, just scrub. We need a sharp stick, she says. She points her torch into the scrub. Find us a stick quick. In you pop, she says.

No way, it's dark, says Jordy.

I look up at them, but their faces are dark too.

Tommo, in you pop.

Okay, I say.

The bushes make scary shapes in the light. I step and push through the bush. The leaves scratch my arms. But there, in the light from the torch, is a perfect stick from a big tree. I pick it up and it's smooth and beautiful in my hands. I laugh. It is obviously not from here. It feels magic. I carry it out above my head.

Look, I say.

Wow, it's perfect, she says. I can tell she's grinning even though I can't see her face. Come on, she says and takes my hand. Our hands go sweaty together. She steps down the path to the beach and we move with the pool of her light. The slippery soft sand is still holding the heat of the day. We stand at the edge of the water and Loretta shines the torch out there. Here, she says, where there's a reef and rocks that hook out into the water it's shallow and flat. It's perfect, she says.

Really? I say.

It looks dark, says Jordy.

It's supposed to be dark, it's got to be dark. Can only catch them on a dark moon. They slip up into the shallows, swimming under the sand, she says. She makes her arms and fingers like frilly fins and I laugh.

What? says Jordy.

It's true. They've got both eyes on the top side of their body. When they're little they look like normal fish with an eye on each side, but as they grow one eye starts travelling to the other side. They're easy prey when they're all wonky. When they're done they put their eyeless side to the sand so they can swim under it. It's true. Your Pa showed me, she says.

Really? I say.

Yeah. Why don't you believe me?

I look out at the dark ocean. With the little knife she cuts a few curls of bark off the end of the stick. Tests the sharpness of the stick, cuts more. She slips the knife back into her pocket.

What now? says Jordy.

We go in, she says. She steps out of her thongs and into the water. The pool of light gets further away, and Jordy and I, we're still standing on the sand in the dark.

Come on, she says, her voice coming from the sea.

I leave my thongs at the water's edge and walk towards the sound of the waves slapping against her calves in the shallows.

The tide is on the turn. They'll be coming in across the shallows in a minute, she says. All three of us stand there, feet underwater. It's so shallow it's like we're standing on the surface of the ocean.

You got to look for faces, she says, for the eyes. She points two fingers at her own shadowy face.

I grab at a bit of her shirt and hold on, the cotton warm and dry in my hand. The wind is whipping at us. It sucks Jordy's singlet around him. I'm looking hard into the circle of the torchlight but all I can see is the pattern of the sand, which looks like how clouds go in an afternoon sky. I can't see a face.

You got to spear 'em, she says. Tie 'em to a line and drag 'em behind you, so you can spear more.

But we ain't got a spear, Loretta, says Jordy.

She brandishes the stick. But we got to find one first. Just look for the eyes, she says.

Loretta walks into the black and I lose hold of her shirt. I look around for Jordy but after staring into the torchlight for so long I can't see nothing. I feel something shift beneath my feet and I step away thinking I am standing on a face.

Jordy? I say.

I walk towards the torchlight but with my next step I'm in water up to my chest and it's rushing much quicker. Waves slap hard and quick against my face. I try to stand still against the current.

Loretta, Loretta, I say. It's as if my voice is being swallowed by the sky. I can see the Southern Cross and the Saucepan and the stars feel like home. Loretta, I say. I'm too deep. I'm worried about sharks, the one that was going to eat Jordy. I'm worried one is swimming this channel looking for a feed, just like us. Loretta, I say, but I realise I'm whispering because I'm scared. I don't want to move in case it gets deeper. I hold my arms up above the water. The waves slap my palms. The air is still hot, but my legs feel cold. Loretta, I try to say louder. I can hear the squeak of panic in my voice. Jordy, I say and look around for him, but it's too dark and Loretta's torch is a spot of light far away. Jordy? I slip forward, deeper. My arms are under. I take a breath of water as I slip. It's quiet and cold. I try to tell my limbs to swim but it's like I've forgotten how to. I fall deeper. I can see the top of the water like a new sky above me. My eyes sting in the salt. I feel heavy as stone. I reach my hand up towards the surface and another hand, warm and real, pulls me up.

I feel sand under my feet. I climb up it. I'm all wet now. I spit salt water and shudder.

Are you okay? says Jordy.

Yeah. He's got both my arms tight in his hands and I try to pull free, but he won't let me.

Okay? he says.

Okay.

I'm shaking with cold. I laugh into the shallows, but it's the kind of laugh that hurts. The wind turns every wet bit I have to cold. My shirt's sucked up on me, I try unstick it. Jordy lets go.

This way, he says.

He walks away, not checking to see if I'm following. I'm quick as a dog at his heels. We reach the hard sand and step out of the water. My hands are still out, like I'm a tightrope walker. I make them go down to my sides. The circle of torch is still way out and moving slowly. We sit on the beach, waiting for a long while for Loretta to come back to shore. I'm completely dry when the rising tide eventually pushes her back in. She doesn't have the stick anymore and the rope is tangled around her arms. She lights us both with the torch, shining it in our eyes.

Tom nearly drowned, says Jordy.

I couldn't see any, she says.

You're blinding me, he says.

She hangs the torch at the end of her hand lighting one little bit of sand. The torch is dull.

Not even one, she says.

Did you hear me? Tom nearly drowned.

I'm okay. I'm okay, I say.

You don't even care, he says.

Come on, I'm tired, she says.

She walks away and we follow, the sand making white socks on my feet. It feels like a dream anyway.

9

In the morning I can't find Jordy. I go stand in the middle of the gravel road. The air is a haze of salt. I suck a breath in to see if I can taste it. I can taste dust. The screen door snaps shut and the awning flaps, making a sound like gunshot. I jump and swing around, but there's no one there. I look over at Nev's caravan but it doesn't look like there's anyone there either. The awning snaps again. I slip off the road, and walk around so that I'm looking at Nev's caravan from the back, with the desert behind me. I hear a generator click on and whirr. I walk closer and step over the white border of rocks. My heart is jumping into my throat. The dirt looks like it has been swept.

Before I get close enough to look up into the hanging buoys, Nev and Jordy walk around the corner. They stop but they don't see me straight away. They're saying something, but the wind whips their words away. Nev grabs a hold of Jordy's arm and pulls him in, close. Jordy sees me. Jordy steps away. Nev lets go. He sees me and crosses his arms. I notice the blurred smudge of tattoos on his forearms. It could be a naked lady and an eagle with its wings extended.

What are you doing out here? Nev says.

Nothing, I say.

Oh yeah? He raises an eyebrow at me and walks up the steps, into the caravan.

What are you doing? I say to Jordy.

Nothing, he says. He's got a tan in the shape of the singlet already, a white strip on his shoulders, permanent. On my shoulders I've got freckles, a whole starry sky of them.

Hey, I say to him.

What? he goes.

It's hot, I say.

Yeah, he goes.

The screen door opens and Nev is standing above us with a tinnie in one hand and a jar of liquorice allsorts in the other. He throws the jar at me. Steps down and collapses into a chair. Jordy takes the jar and undoes the lid, putting his hand in there. He fills his mouth with lollies and chews. They're all stuck together and I get a clump of them out. In my mouth they're rubbery as tyre and sweet.

Not bad, eh, says Nev and takes a long swig of beer. I take a good look at his blurred tattoos. Lean over, pull the wrinkles apart and make the skin smooth. It ain't a lady. It's the face of a boy on Nev's arm. It looks like a copy of a school photo. He looks awkward, with teeth missing, his hair too neat and combed weird. The wrinkles fall back. I can see his face in the blur of the wrinkles now that I know he's hiding in there.

Tom, hisses Jordy.

What? I say.

Nev looks up at me and his eyelids are pink as a dog's tongue.

You reckon you can just do whatever you want without asking? he says.

No, I say, no. I didn't mean nothing.

Get out of here, get, he says, get.

Let's go, Tom, says Jordy.

Why? I say.

Come on, let's go.

No.

Let's go, he hisses at me and grabs my arm. I drop the jar of allsorts. Sticky black squares in the dirt.

Jordy. I look up at Nev and he steps closer towards us. I try to pick up the jar but Jordy pulls me out of the yard, past the border of white rocks. The buoys sway in the wind, the heavy glass globes rocking back and forth on their ropes. Jordy pulls me towards the road.

You shouldn't snoop around, he says to me, still with a tight grip on my arm. I wrench it from him.

You're not the boss of me.

I am.

What were you doing with him anyway?

I wasn't doing anything.

Did he give you anything else?

No.

You shouldn't hang around him.

It's better that I do.

What do you mean?

Do you reckon Loretta's in there? he says. The caravan is in front of us now. Rusted and looking like it's going to fall apart any second.

Probly.

It'd be hot in there.

Yeah, I say, giving up.

We walk past our caravan to the beach. I look over my shoulder back at Nev's but there is no one there, no one watching us. I can taste the liquorice in my mouth. We walk through the soft sand to the water, the hard wet edge, then towards the point. Jordy walks ahead of me, even when I try to catch up, he's always one step ahead. I give up, and walk slowly, and he slows too. I see a hermit crab creep from the rocks. It stands out in the open for a bit and I see that its shell isn't a shell. Its soft body is encased in a bit of PVC pipe. It slips away under a rock.

Did you see that?

What? says Jordy.

That crab.

No.

I turn away from him and run back up the beach. I sink into the hot, soft sand. It's like it's grabbing at my feet. I run up the track. I open the caravan door. Loretta's lying on her bed. She opens her eyes. I can see the sweat on her. I don't say anything. Grab all the shells from the windowsill. Run back to the beach and dump them back on the sand, near where the hermit crab was.

Sorry, I say to it. Sorry.

Jordy says, Are you retarded?

But I ignore him. I wait there for ages, for the crab to come out and change into a proper shell. Of course it doesn't.

I open the door to the caravan and Loretta is still there on the bed, curled up in a ball.

I'm hungry, I say loudly. She doesn't answer. I'm hungry, Loretta. Mum, I say.

She sits up and gives me a look from beneath her messy hair. She inches over to the edge of the bed, You want to go to town? she says. We'll go to town. She stands up, smoothing her T-shirt. She pours herself a big glass of water and I watch it go down her throat as she drinks. The container is nearly empty. Come on, she says, grabbing the keys from the bench. Jordy is sitting outside.

We're going to town, she says.

Can I stay here? says Jordy.

No, says Loretta, you can't stay here.

What are we gunna get? I say.

Whatever you want.

Why can't I stay? says Jordy.

'Cos, you can't. End of discussion.

Shotgun, I say and jump to Bert's front door grinning, but Jordy ignores me. He goes to the back door of Bert, pops it open and slumps into the back seat. He digs a space for his feet in among the rubbish.

Let's go, eh, says Loretta and she leans over the gearstick and opens my door from the inside. I get in. The seat cover feels rough. I grip the armrest as Loretta drives too fast out of there. I turn around and can't see the caravan disappearing for the dust. Jordy's head is hanging to his chest.

Jordy, I go.

What? he says but doesn't look me in the eye.

Nothing.

Sitting in the front, it's like the road is too close, coming up to meet me.

Our trolley is yellow with Black and Gold. We line up behind two surfers with wide shoulders and no shirts. Loretta jiggles on the spot.

Mum, Jordy says and she spins around.

What? she says too quiet.

Nothing, he says too loud and smirks.

The men look around at us. Their hips jut out over the tops of their shorts. They have a line of hair to their bellybuttons. They look Loretta up and down. The lady at the counter beeps their big bag of chips and lemonades through. I look at my feet, ashamed, but I don't know why.

Six-ninety, the lady says to them. How are you? she says to us.

Fine, says Loretta. Wait for me outside, she says to me and Jordy. Jordy pushes past me, and I squeeze past Loretta.

Outside I see the men in a panel van. They've got their arms hanging out the windows. Time goes so slow that every second stretches long into the afternoon, long enough to reach the slit of the horizon. One of them takes a drag on his cigarette and flicks it, still lit, towards us.

Come on, says Jordy.

What? I go.

He walks away, out of the carpark and up the wide empty street.

Hey, hey, I say. He ignores me and I can see the points of his shoulder blades sticking out his back through the singlet.

What? You don't have to come, he says.

Hey, wait up, I say.

Just shut up for once.

We walk past the fish and chip shop. My mouth waters from the smell of salt and vinegar. Jordy's walking to the highway, which is just the main street of the town. It runs all the way out of it, north. Jordy kicks a bottle cap along the pavement as he walks. It makes a tinkly sound. I run up in front of him and kick the cap before he gets to it.

Oi, he says, and trots after me.

It's weird how the town just finishes, I say, stopping.

He walks in front again, without checking to see if I'm following. He's left the bottle cap. I stoop down and get it, put it in my pocket. I flick it around and around in there, feeling the smooth top, the plastic inside and the sharp ridges with my fingertips.

Jordy keeps walking. There are shacks but their windows are half smashed out or so dirty they're black. I can hear a truck and, looking up, I see it's huge, rising up out of the hazy line between sky and road. It takes ages to get to us. Then, as it passes, the wind is so strong it pulls my hair and shirt, and tries hard to suck me in towards it.

Jordy, I say to his back, how long do you reckon it takes between when you see a car and when it gets to us?

I don't know.

But what do you *reckon*?

He turns around. I nearly bump into him. He puts his hand up in front of his forehead and makes the shape of an L – loser.

Maybe we should go back to town, I say. He turns around and keeps walking the way we've been going.

Jordy, do you reckon our dad's on a prawn trawler?

No, he says. I don't reckon our dad's on a prawn trawler.

He could be, though, don't you reckon?

I told you, how do you know my dad is your dad?

I take a deep breath, throw away the bottle cap and keep walking.

Hey, he says, hey, Tom. He touches my shoulder and I shrug him off.

Get lost, I say. I can hear his footsteps behind me. I look back and I see the smudge of a yellow car coming. It's Loretta, I say.

He turns around and grabs me, pulls me towards one of the falling-down houses. His fingers dig into my arm.

Stop it, I say. Stop it.

Come on.

Jordy, it's her.

Come on.

You're hurting me.

He pulls me around the back of the house, through the open door. My heart beats right into the roof of my mouth. It stinks bad of cat piss in here. The floorboards creak. I feel ready to fall through them. There's newspaper in the corner of the room and the place is dirty as, but there's an old hat still hooked on the wall, like the owners just stepped out the door, like they'll be back.

I hear a car pull into the driveway. We're at the window. Shit, says Jordy.

But it's Loretta, I say.

I know it's Loretta, you retard, he says. This close I can see the flecks of colour in his eyes.

I am *not* a retard, I say.

Shh, he says.

Guys, this is no fun, she says from outside.

He sighs, gets up, and I follow him out onto the veranda. The wooden boards sag onto a garden made of weeds. Loretta is out there, sitting on the old orange and green swing set. Her bum squished into the kid-sized swing.

Hey, she says.

We don't say anything. I step down to the ground. I kick into the dirt and just under the surface is the leg of a plastic doll and faded blocks of Lego. The earth gives them up for me.

You two wanna give me a heart attack? she says and jumps off the swing. She walks back to Bert and we follow her. The car is full of shopping bags. Jordy gets in the front and slams the door shut.

Hey, I had shotgun, I say.

He ignores me and Loretta. Sits there in silence. I get in the back and try slam the door harder than him. Loretta accelerates away. I look back at the house. The black windows are like gaps between teeth.

Bert's engine tick ticks. We all sit in the car too long, looking at the caravan until Jordy opens his door, gets out and walks down to the toilet. I look across to Loretta and she tucks her hair behind her ears. The hair falls out and she tucks it back again. When she looks up there's surprise in her eyes. It's like she has forgotten I'm there.

Hey, she says.

Hey, I say.

We get out of Bert. I let my hand run along the dirty metal, leave a long stripe on him. Loretta stands outside the caravan and lights a cigarette. She's fidgeting. She blows smoke and doesn't sit down.

I open Bert's back door and get a bag of shopping out. It's heavy, the plastic cuts into my hand. I carry it to the door of the caravan and nudge my way past Loretta. I push against the door with my shoulder in the way I've figured out will open it. Inside it's hot. I chuck the bag on the table and cans roll out of it.

I go get a water from the container and it's nearly empty, right down to the bit that's kind of brown. The other container is empty too. I sip it and it's hot, but I still drink it in one long gulp. I wipe my sweat off onto my shirt and leave my glass with all the other dirty ones at the sink. I stumble down the metal steps, out.

There's a woman in bike pants and a Winners are Grinners T-shirt out there. She's got a little girl on her hip. She stands just outside the square of shade. I jump to see a stranger there. I stand still as a statue. Look at Loretta out of the corner of my eye.

Hi, says the lady.

Loretta says, Hi, from behind her hair.

I saw the sign, she says, the other day. You still doing that, cutting hair?

Yeah. No, says Loretta.

'Cos, she says, adjusting the girl on her hip, my hair is just hopeless. She puts her hand up and scrunches her fingers into it. I don't get a chance to go to the hairdresser, you know, she says. Not with this little fella.

The little girl puts her thumb in her mouth. The woman smiles a smile that makes her look pretty. Loretta flicks her fringe out of her eyes and for a second she looks just like Jordy. The smiling lady looks at me.

What's your name? she says to me.

Tom, I say.

That's a *cooool* name, she says.

I laugh, try to stop my grin.

This is Jenny, she says. The little girl hides her face in her mum's shirt. Where are you guys from? she says.

East, says Loretta.

Oh yeah, she says, I've never been over that way. Is it nice?

Yeah, says Loretta, it's nice.

The ocean's a different colour, I say.

Really? the lady says. Isn't that something.

Loretta comes closer to me, puts her hand on my shoulder. It ain't that different, she says.

Yes, it is, I say.

New Year's tomorrow, the lady says.

Is it? says Loretta.

Yeah, says the lady. It's easy to lose track of the days, isn't it?

I guess so, says Loretta.

The lady adjusts the little girl on her hip and after a long stretch of silence says, So you're not cutting hair?

Nah, says Loretta.

Okay, she says, see ya then.

She walks away and I can hear the little girl giggling. The lady swings her around and onto the other hip. Loretta takes her hand from my shoulder.

Loretta, the water's nearly empty.

What? she says.

We forgot about getting water.

Just be quiet, she says. Just be quiet for one minute, okay. She slumps down into a chair and flicks her cigarette lighter on and off in her hand. Lights another cigarette and ignores me.

I leave her there, walk down to the toilet. I can hear the corrugated iron door clang, clang again. In the morning the tin clicks and ticks as it heats up. It's surrounded by a big, dirty, sandy circle. I look in through a nail hole in the iron and see Jordy brushing flies from his face. He wobbles on the drop-toilet seat. There's a can of sawdust next to him and a toilet roll on a wire but it looks like nothing is coming. Jordy stands up, closes the lid of the toilet – it's the top of a can of paint – pulls up his shorts. He don't need the toilet paper 'cos he ain't done nothing. I don't make a move, just stand quiet beside the dunny. The door clangs open.

Hey, he says, what are you doing?

Nothing.

You spying on me again?

No.

You are.

I am not.

You're a bloody pervert.

I am not.

Say, I'm a pervert.

No.

Well, you are. He walks back towards the caravan.

Jordy, let's go to the beach.

He looks me over, then keeps walking back to the caravan.

Maybe you'll never poo again, I say.

He turns, walks back, punches me hard in the arm.

Shut. Up. he says. A punch for each word.

Loretta's not outside. I trail behind Jordy. He goes inside the caravan. I can feel the heat from the sun on the awning. I hear the crying then, a soft mewling like a kitten makes. I can't see through the screen, it's black. I open it and Jordy's standing there. He looks too big for the space. Loretta's at the table crying, our blankets at her feet. For a moment, because it's so hot and dry, the strangest thing is just that her face is wet.

part two

10

The sound comes into my sleep as part of a dream. When I realise I'm awake I can't remember the dream, just the sound of Bert's engine vibrating through it. The sound of the engine is real, though. I can hear Bert outside, the sounds he makes before he's ready to drive. Closer is the sound of Jordy's breaths. I can tell by their length that he's still deep asleep. Opening my eyes I see his arm caught under him. It'll be dead. Pins and needles.

I wipe sweat off my face and peel myself from the seat. Loretta's not in her bed. I am much too slow with sleep. She's in Bert. Bare feet on the sandy floor. I hear Bert leaving too early, before his engine is warm, like she can sense I'm awake. I open the screen door and there's only dust already. I start counting to one hundred. If she comes back by the time I reach one hundred it will be okay. I can still hear the rumble of Bert on the corrugations. I reach one hundred. I hold my breath. The morning is clear. The sky is blue. Here it's always blue and bigger than I thought possible. I realise I have been gripping the door. I unclaw my hand from it. Along my palm is a deep red stripe. I try bring the blood back in there.

Jordy, Jordy, I say. I rub the sand from my feet. It makes a rough shushing sound. Jordy. I can't hear Bert anymore. Jordy. Not even the low growl the cars make when they're still ages away down the road.

Yeah, he says, mumbling into his pillow. He's too sleepy to be mean. He shifts himself and releases his arm. I watch him clenching and unclenching his fist.

I think Loretta's gone, I say. He's very still. He sits up, moves over to the edge of the seat. I can see the outline of his singlet tan, and there's a shaft of sunlight that slashes across his chest.

Really? he says. Rubs his eyes, gouging the sleep out of them.

I wait for him to yell at me, 'cos I reckon that's probably what's going to happen next. I try get every bit of sand from my foot, but when it's clean I have to rest it on the floor and I feel the thousands of grits there, back again already.

He shakes his head like he's shaking a dream from it. Is she gone to get water? he says.

I look over at the big plastic containers, still on the bench and hollow. Nup, I say.

He gets up and takes a cup from the sink and fills it with water. He has to lean the container right over.

Can I have one? I say.

Get it yourself, he says and gulps his water down. Some

trickles down his chin and onto his chest. I push past him, find the least dirty cup and hold the container in my arms. It's so light I can only get one cup out of it.

Okay, he says to himself.

There is a line of ants coming from the roof of the caravan, from the window that pops like a tank's opening. A black line of them, as if drawn there with a lead pencil. I open the cupboard, start pulling things out. A can opener, an old aerosol that looks like it's made of rust, a blunt knife that I test on my thumb. There are used plastic plates together in the sink, the colour of a dirty rainbow.

What are you doing? he says.

I don't know, I say. I don't know what I'm doing. Hang my arms to my sides, lick my chapped lips and look to the ceiling like there is an answer there. Jordy pushes past me and out the screen door. The door screams its scream. I follow him out.

What should we do, I say.

Nothing, we're not going to do nothing, Jordy says.

So you reckon she'll be back?

Yeah, he says but he don't look anywhere near my eyes when he says it.

I'm bored.

So. What.

The heat is crouched down around us. I look over at Nev's van, but I can't see no one there.

Maybe he'll take us again, I say and motion to the van across the road.

No, says Jordy loudly.

But he took us last time.

No, says Jordy. Just shut up. Let me think.

I'm hungry.

Well, have something to eat then, he says sarcastically, rolling his words at me. I hear a magpie warbling in the distance, singing as if through water. I go into the caravan, there's Weetbix. There's no bowls in the cupboards, though. In the sink I find one that doesn't look too bad and wipe it out with a dirty tea towel. I sprinkle powdered milk and fine white sugar until I can't see the Weetbix anymore. I hold the water container high and drip the last drips of water over the bowl. The drips make damp spots. I go back outside and sit on the steps, swat the flies from me. Spoon the dry cereal into my mouth. It takes me a really long time to chew and swallow. The sugar crunches and encases my mouth.

We'll just wait for her, he says.

Okay, I say and suck on the sugar.

She'll be back. He gets up and walks down the path towards the toilet, his head down against the light.

Good luck, I say. He gives me the finger without turning around and a laugh escapes my sugar mouth. Then I remember Loretta and there's worry inside me, vibrating. I look over at Nev's caravan. It looks like a face with two blank window eyes and a door mouth. The grass sways in the breeze.

I walk across the road. Step over the border of rocks, pause to see if anything bad happens. I can't see anyone down the road, left or right. I step up Nev's front path to the door. I stand on my tiptoes and try and look in the window.

Oi, he says.

I swing around, trip and scrape my arm on the tinny windowsill.

Hello, I say. He's got a rod in his hand, it bounces over his head, moving even though he is still. I smell rotten prawns.

What'd I tell ya? he says. Stay away. His face is brown, shiny and weathered like them washed-up coconuts covered in husk. Get out of my yard, get, he says.

But.

No buts.

But.

What did I say?

Walking past him I see a dead fish in his bucket, the scales still there, shiny, and at the mouth of the fish, blood.

I'll gut you, he says and makes a motion with his hand from bellybutton to neck – splitting himself right down his middle.

I run. I look back and stumble, but he's no longer there. The caravan looks exactly the same, except now I know that he's somewhere behind the square windows. I run into our caravan and jump on Loretta's bed – safe.

The scrape on my arm is red, but there's no blood. I spit on my finger and smooth it over the scratch. I wait for Jordy for a long time, but he doesn't come back.

The toilet door is open and Jordy's not there. I close it and hook the string back on the nail. Walk the path over the dune to the beach. The ocean is there, big and stupid. The beach is busy with fishing. I look for Jordy and see him slouching further down the beach. I slide down the dune, my feet sinking deep in the soft sand, and walk towards him.

I've been looking for you.

He rolls his eyes at me. Whatever, he says.

But Jordy –

Leave me alone, alright, he says.

A wave, with a line of spit-white foam at its edge, runs up to my feet. He walks away but I don't let him go. I follow five steps behind. I feel our caravan, empty as a cicada shell behind the dune. I smell the stench of fish.

Quit following me, he says.

I'm not following you. I'm going this way.

I said, fuck off.

You fuck off, I say, but there's no force in my words.

We're both standing on the hard edge of the beach, alone. Jordy walks across the sand and back up the path to the caravans. I sit down and hold my knees and draw my fingers through the sand. When I look back for him the dunes have swallowed him up. I uncurl from a ball and walk the other way, past the jetty, towards the river mouth.

Here is the only place where the scrub turns tall. There are trees along the riverbank but there's no water. The bank crumbles at my feet. It feels cooler in the scrappy shade, but there's the hot hum of insects here. Looking up I can see the sky through the leaves and great big hunks of dead wood still standing. It makes me dizzy and I steady myself against the heat. I can see a gum across the dry riverbed and one of its branches is shiny like something rubbed for good luck. There's a rope hanging out there, thick, with two big knots, one for your hands and one for your feet. There ain't no water, though, it swings into nothing.

I slide down the riverbank to where the roots hang out over the sand. They're dusty. I climb in under there, hug my legs to my chest and stare at the spiders' webs that look like they're holding it all together. It's cool under the roots. The wide sandy river shimmers in the heat, almost like water. I get out of there.

The sand slithers over my thongs and burns my feet. There's a line of ants right across the river. The rope dangles above me and I'm in the shade again. I lift my hand, see if I can touch it, but it's out of reach. I use the exposed roots to climb up the bank and then it's easy to climb the gum, its trunk sloping out, reaching over the river. I lie out on the smoothed-off bark. I hang my arms and legs over the branch like I reckon a sloth would and I feel the smoothness against my cheek.

I spit over the edge. Cockatoos whirl around me, and one lands on the limb opposite. Then they're all landed, screaming yellow. A cockatoo looks at me with one eye, and all the others are screeching, jumping up and down, their heads bobbing, like they're laughing. They rip leaves apart and the shreds drop on me. I scream back. They fly up and all of them in a smooth arc land back in the tree to laugh at me again. I nearly fall off the slippery branch so I inch my way back down the limb to the bank. I find a good stick and switch the grass as I walk, following a trail that's been flattened in the dry grass. The paperbarks are ripped and clawed. I dig my fingers into them as I pass, try to find the hard inside the tree.

There's a pool of black water. I fling the stick down the bank, jump after it, jarring my legs. Pa says that heels are like a crab's shell, hard but secretly fragile, that they can shatter into a million pieces, just like if you tap a crab's shell with a hammer. I always try to jump soft.

There are rings in the dirt all down to the water where it has shrunk and shrunk. The hottest days have the biggest space between the rings, like years on a cut-down tree trunk. I find a rock and throw it into the water and the wake circles out to the edge of the pool to meet my toes. My feet sink into the slimy soup and I feel little things slip over my toes. I step in further, hold my arms out to steady myself.

The black water thrashes and I see the sharp triangle of a shark fin, then the water is still. I stumble back and fall, cracking through the dried mud. I perch on my heels and wait, but the surface of the water is unbroken. I'm so silent a kangaroo with its hop-crawl comes and drinks from the water on the opposite side. I'm not as tall as a kangaroo. My legs begin to cramp. I stand and point my stick at the kangaroo like it's a rifle. The kangaroo faces me, chest puffed out, before it bounds away. Bang, bang, bang. I shoot that kangaroo dead. I poke the stick in the water and I can see something shifting. It's a good k of dry riverbed to the sea, and I don't know if a shark could survive that long out of water. The sky is huge with only a fart of a cloud near the horizon. The pool of water shrinks.

The mud has dried on my legs, but it comes off when I scratch it. I stand up and follow my footsteps in the dirt, back up to the bank, the stick resting on my shoulder.

Walking back over the dunes I see the caravan. It's like the grass has grown further up around it. There's no Bert. I aim my stick and blow out the windows of the caravan with it. I go look in the front door and Jordy's not there. I lean my stick against the hot tin, open the screen door to get a water. I lift the containers, they're light as balloons full of hot breath.

Jordy? I say, looking around for signs he's been here. His school shirt is down there, under the table, curled and discarded like snakeskin. Jordy? I say.

The step creaks with my weight and I let the screen door snap shut. I can't see anyone over the road, but the ute is there, waiting patient at the side of Nev's caravan. I walk around the side of his caravan, dragging my stick behind me. The shadow of the caravan looks sharp enough to cut. There's no one out there. The glass buoys twist in the slight breeze. I stand on my tiptoes to look through a salty window. I wait for my eyes to adjust to the darkness. The hot tin of the caravan is burning my palm. I realise I've been blocking the hum of the generator out. The sound has been there all the time. I hear it now and I can smell the diesel belch.

My eyes come good. Jordy's chest looks concave. His fringe hangs way over his face. It's like he's standing there alone even though there's Nev with his pants off, sitting on the vinyl chair, looking at him, jerking off. Me standing there, my hand burning onto the tin, like if I moved it I'd rip the skin right off my palm. Nev's thighs look totally hairless and whiter than everything else. He's still got his thongs on his feet. He's gripping Jordy's arm. But he lets go, wipes his face with his forearm and turns his watery eyes to me. I see his penis slowly droop. I see the red marks where his hand has been on Jordy's skin. Nev's eyes look full of tears. His head bumps to his chest. Jordy looks at me. He closes his eyes and it's like a cloud passing over the sun. I rip my hand from the tin and run.

11

I can feel the heat of an ant bite blooming on my neck. I'm way in deep under the roots of the riverbank. I dig away at the surface sand until it's cooler and I put my hands there, feeling the secret temperature. I can hear my breath, and I try make it come slower. I count them. Where my hands are becomes hot. I dig my fingers in deeper until I can feel hard dirt right up under my fingernails.

I see Jordy's feet land with a cloud of dust. They're chopped off at the calves. He has the skinniest ankles ever. I'm quiet. I see them twist around as he's looking. He starts to walk away. I've lost count of my breaths. I make a noise that is a cough or a sob. His feet pause, he comes back, leans right over and I see his face. Two dark eyes. He crawls in under the roots, their ends are as soft and fine as spiders' webs. His pockets tinkle.

There's not enough room for us both under here. Little bits of the ceiling crumble. I rub my eyes. He's holding a soda machine like the one Pa had on the liquor cabinet. It's old with a silver handle and wire mesh. He's trying not to sit too close. His legs are stretching out into the sun.

Go away, I say, but it comes out as a whisper.

He pulls little silver bulbs out of his pockets. Here, he says and passes the soda machine to me.

I don't want it, I say.

He presses it into my hands, but my hands don't work and it falls and rolls in the sand.

Where did you get it? I say. He pushes the machine back into my hands and everything now is covered with a fine silt of sand. But I just hold it.

Look, I'll show you, he says and grabs it back off me.

He pierces a bulb and then wraps his singlet over the spout of the machine and presses the leaver down. He sucks it in, holds it, then blows it out slowly. His face is too close to mine, and under here it's too dark for me to see what's happening but I think he closes his eyes and leans back for a couple of seconds. Then he's laughing.

Here, he says. Here.

He passes me the machine again, and a new little silver bulb. I put my Pooh shirt over the spout, pierce the bulb and then breathe in a huge breath. My lungs go freezing cold. I try breathe it back out as quick as possible but then it feels like I'm falling into the riverbank. The earth opens and closes again over the top of me and I'm in there with the roots and the bones and the spiders. There's humming in my brain and even though I'm in there way too deep it's okay.

I hear cicadas first. The tendrils of roots come back into focus, and I feel the sand under my fingertips and Jordy beside me. I'm sitting there exactly the same as before. I gasp and a tear escapes. I feel it run down my cheek and drop to my leg. Jordy grabs the soda machine from my limp hand. I look at him suck it through his singlet with a loud hiss and close his eyes. The silver bulb falls. They're like spent machine-gun cartridges. I feel weird and cool on the inside. There is a headache waiting to boom, but it's hiding in the back of my head for now.

I wriggle out. Tendrils brush against my face. I go look at the water that's thick and smells nothing like I expect the bottom of a river to smell. I feel Jordy come stand beside me.

There's a shark in there, I say. I point to the water. Jordy doesn't say anything, but I hear him sigh. There is, I say.

There is not, he says reluctantly.

Go for a swim then.

He shrugs his shoulders as if to say, whatever.

I raise my eyebrows at him. There is a shark.

He looks at me, then slips his thongs off his feet. He jumps up and down. The sand is hot. He walks on tiptoe to the edge of the water then curls his toes into the mud.

This is fucken gross, he says. But his feet are in the water now and he's walking deeper.

Hey, I say, there really is a shark. Really. He rolls his eyes at me and walks deeper. Jordy, there's a shark. Stop. He rolls his eyes again. Come out, come out, come out. He walks in deeper. I look around for anything to chuck in the water. Jordy, I say. I stand on the edge of the mud. A little lizard slithers away through the muck and Jordy flinches, then walks deeper. The dried mud cracks under my feet. I lean down and, keeping my eyes on him, like if I look away it will get him, I feel around in the mud for anything to throw. I find a small branch, the bark crumbles under my fingers. I pull it from the mud and throw it past Jordy, into the water. The black water rises up and the fin breaks the surface. Everything is fast. The shark thrashes in the shallows and Jordy stumbles back and onto his bum in the mud. The black water creeps up into his shirt. I don't laugh. He pushes himself further out of there, leaving gouges.

Shit, he says, and lets a little laugh escape his chest.

We got to catch it, I say. But I mean, we got to save it.

Gulls circle above us. They're eyeing us off. The sound of the generator makes me queasy. I can see Nev's buoys turning in the wind. We're down in the scrub. Little sticks dig into me.

I don't want you to, I say.

Just be quiet, he says, it'll be okay. He's not there.

But – and I feel an ache in my throat that's more than being thirsty, or crying.

I'm just going to get some fishing gear, he says.

No, I say.

He's not there.

But what if he comes? I start to cry. I'm trying so hard not to, but Jordy's there like nothing's happened. I see my tears land in big drops in the dust. They just sit on the top of the sand, perfect, whole and round.

Do you want to get the shark or what? Don't be a fucken baby, he says. But he puts his hand on my back and rubs three circles there before standing up and walking into the yard. His long hair blows out. I put my head in my hands and don't look. I can see my feet. They're orange with dust. Ants crawl over my toes. I count my breaths, and I'm up to eighty-seven when I hear bushes rustling. I look up, holding eighty-seven in. The sun is so high in the sky that Jordy doesn't even cast me into shade. Our shadows are there, cowering at our feet.

Come on, he says. Quick.

He's got a handful of sparkling metal fish and a handline threaded on his arm like a bangle. A gaff hanging from his wrist. I trail him. We walk back down to the beach. Crabs scuttle at my feet.

He's going to know it was us that took it, I say.

I know, but it doesn't matter. He won't do anything, says Jordy.

How do you know?

He just won't.

You're crazy, I say. Jordy just shrugs.

Maybe I just know, he says.

At the mouth of the river a pied oystercatcher flashes its bright red beak at us, then flies away. The sand is wide and flat here where briny seawater pools. We walk past where the water stops and the river sand begins, until we reach the shark. We stand in the sun, the mud drying and cracking around us. I'm thirsty. My tongue is starting to get fat and thick. The lure shimmers and swims, flapping its silver fins. The fish is so pretty it could lure all the birds from the sky. The pool of water shrinks.

I'm hot, I say.

Jordy ignores me. I watch him tie the lure to the handline and then swing it in a circle before letting it fly, the line unravelling as if from his open palm. The fish flies into the river sand on the other side and the line blows away. Jordy reels the line back in. I run around and get the lure. It glints at me, lets me know it's there. I brush dust off it, feel the sharp tips of the hooks. I throw it to Jordy and he jumps aside.

Hey, he says and picks up the lure.

Remember how Pa says, the rabbit goes around the burrow, then down the hole, I say.

He threads the line through the eye then makes a circle for the burrow and threads the rabbit through it, down the burrow, and pulls it tight. He chucks it into the soupy water and winds it back in quickly.

Get the gaff ready, he says.

He chucks it again and again but nothing happens. Only the ripples of water circle out.

Maybe we need some berley, some blood, I say.

He looks at me like he's measuring how much I've got to spare. But the shark takes the bait then and the handline nearly rips from him. He grabs a hold of it and winds it in, his feet digging deep into the mud. He's sweating, his hair sticks to his face. Bits of the shark start to show. It throws black water at us. It'd be hungry, I reckon. It must have eaten every fish in there and maybe even things that came to drink.

Get the gaff, says Jordy. He's straining, his arm is going to pop out of its socket, but I don't want to get the gaff 'cos I don't want to hurt it. I see the square snout. I see one of its eyes looking at me before it twists and turns and is all grey skin and fins again. I think it looks a bit like the face of a dog. The gaff is hooked at the end of my arm and I reach in and pull it through the jaw of the little gummy. Pull it up onto the sand. It flicks around, snapping and twisting.

Quick, quick, quick, Jordy, quick, quick. I'm yelling, jumping up and down with the shark at the end of the gaff.

What, what the fuck, what? he screams back at me.

We got to get it to the ocean, quick.

It's too far.

I start pulling it towards the river mouth, dragging it along by the gaff, leaving a line of blood and filling the shark with sand. It's hard to pull because the shark is heavy and wild at the end of the hook. Jordy drops the line and tries to grab the tail but it slips out of his hands. The line gets caught by the wind and floats behind us unravelling into blue sky.

Give me the gaff, he says. I hand it to him and he runs, pulling the shark behind him. The shark grazes against my ankles and its skin is rough. I try grab the tail, but the tail is as difficult to grab as a hose turned on full. I fall into the sand and it burns everywhere it touches. I gasp with the shock of the heat, get up.

Wait, Jordy, I say and try to run after him. Wait.

But he's getting away from me. I can see the muscles in his arms, tense and pulling too hard. I run after him. We leave blood behind us.

Be gentle, Jordy. Be careful, I say, catching up to him. Jordy just pulls harder on the shark. I grab its tail and it lets me. Now, we're more walking, stumbling after a while. I don't look back because I'm scared of how little way we've come. My headache booms at me with each step. I can hear Jordy's ragged breath. Then there's the sea. It's so blue it's painful. We fall into the water and Jordy pulls the shark in after us. Blood seeps from the shark's mouth. I wash the sand off its rough, grey skin. Jordy's enormous singlet billows out like a parachute in the water. I hug the shark to me. It doesn't move. The gaff hangs from its lips. The lure in its mouth shines like a new filling. We float in the shallows, on the end of a line, bumping up against each other.

12

Jordy is slick and dark with water.

Is it dead? Little pale fish, the colour of sand, dart around our feet. I see one take a nibble at the shark's lip. The waves rock it back and forth. I've seen when fishermen throw almost-dead fish back. They pull the water through the gills of the limp fish and it comes alive. The gummy bobs in the water.

Yeah, I guess, says Jordy.

Gulls circle overhead. One of them lands on the beach, arches its back, screeches at us. Waves curling around our legs. Jordy reaches down and for a second I think he's going to thump me, but he gets a hold of the tail of the shark and starts pulling it back to the sand. It bares its teeth at me, grinning.

He gets it to the sand, then slumps down beside it, leans back with his hands under his head and closes his eyes.

You killed it, I say. But I know I'm the one who really killed it, because I found it in there and it was me that wanted to catch it, but I say it again, You killed it.

Just shut up, he says.

The bite on my neck is itchy. I dig my fingers into it. I hate you, I say to Jordy, standing above him. He opens his eyes. I saw you before, I say to him.

Whatever, he says, it comes out of his lips in a hiss. He's lying there, still.

I saw, I say. I scratch at the bite on my neck hard.

He sits up, tackles my legs from under me. He gets two of my wrists into one of his hands so he can have the other free to punch my face. I kick up into his belly. I smell his breath, hot and like rotten meat pie. His hair gets in my eyes.

Get off me, I yell at him. He's grimacing so hard his lips crack and I see blood on his teeth. His face is red. The sound of waves breaking.

Don't say anything, he whispers between his bloody teeth, his lips clenched tight. A vein in his forehead is pulsing and sticking out so far that I want to reach up and put my finger on it, feel the pumping of the blood. But he has both my hands. I knee him in the balls and he falls off me. He curls up, groans. When he looks up at me the water reflects in his eyes and makes them shiny blue.

It doesn't matter, Tom, he says.

I look away. We both look at the gummy. He gets up, Come on, he says. He gets the gummy. He hugs it, holding its head in his arms. We'll take it back, he says. Get the tail.

Even though it's a small shark it still has that scary feeling to look at it. It feels as if maybe it could still give me a nip. The

146

hairs on my arms are white with salt. Jordy has a good hold on the gummy. The flies come.

We walk back up the beach, the tail slips. I stumble in the high-tide mark. The seaweed curls and scratches my ankles, tangles my feet. I'm stuck there trying to get out of it and Jordy looks back at me with such a pained expression, his arms full of shark, that I feel like giving up, letting the seaweed keep me and just waiting for the tide to rise.

Come on, he says. I pull myself from the weed. At the dunes we drop the gummy and it gets covered with sand again. He pushes it up the sand and I get above and try pull it up by the head. Trying not to gouge its eyes out. At the top of the dune we hug it again. We walk back towards the caravan. I can smell sausages and kerosene. I can't itch the ant bite on my neck because I'm holding the shark. The gulls are following us, circling high above, and as we get to the caravan they settle on the roof. We get in under the awning and I let the gummy's dry tail drop. Jordy has the head still, he gently lowers it to the ground. The gummy's arm fin is poking up, waving hello. I stare at the place where Bert should be.

She's still not home, I say and look up at Jordy.

Yeah, he says. I hear him breathe out all the way, until he must be totally empty inside. I slump down in the half-broken chair, the gummy at my feet. But from here I can see Nev's caravan. The windows are dark. The front is neat, like he's swept the dirt since this morning. Jordy opens the caravan door and I get up, follow him in. My chair collapses on top of the gummy.

There's an elastic on the windowsill, with her hair still in it. A red singlet under the bed. Blown tissues along the edge of the bed. I finger half a piece of bread that's gone hard left out on the bench.

Are there any chips left? I say.

I dunno, he says.

He sits at the table. I look in the cupboard and inside the big Black and Gold bag there is one packet left – chicken flavour. I reach in and pull the little green packet out and show it to Jordy triumphantly.

Chips, I say. He rubs a space clean on the table and raises his eyebrows at me. I open the chips and stick them one at a time into my mouth. They're so covered in flavour they almost burn. Do ya want one? I say when there's really only crumbs left.

No, he says and rests his head on the table.

I open the screen door and look down at the gummy. There are flies crawling all over its eyes and near its bared rows of teeth. The awning snaps in a new breeze and the air grabs the empty chip packet from my hand. It floats up and over the dune. I go to run after it but it's gone. I tighten the awning, like that's what I'm out there for, pulling it out as hard as I can. The gummy is rotting at my feet.

There's heaps of flies on it, I say loudly so Jordy can hear me inside. I look up and see a lady walking towards me. It's not Loretta because Loretta walks jaunty, like how teenage boys walk. This woman is swaying with a growth on her hip.

I look for somewhere to put the gummy. I grab the chair and it tangles in my arms, snapping me in the mouth. I taste blood.

Jordy, I say. No answer.

I take a hold of the gummy's fin. Roll it over, under the

caravan. The tail catches on the metal step. I shove it and a little triangle of the tail snaps and hangs by a flap of skin. I taste blood and chicken flavouring.

Jordy, I say.

He opens the door and looks out. What? he says. Then – What does she want?

As she walks up we both look at our feet.

Hi, she says.

I can see her feet, her thongs. She starts talking like it's a conversation we've all been having before and she starts right in the middle of it.

She just cries and cries if I don't walk her, she says, but if I walk her she's happy as Larry, aren't you, sweets, happy as Larry. I look up at the tiny girl. The girl gurgles, laughing bubbles of spit. The woman kisses the little girl on the top of her head.

Your mum here? she says. Thought I might try see if she'd reconsider. She touches her hair. About my hair, she says.

I say, Nup, but Jordy speaks over me.

She's gone into town, he says.

And left you two all on your lonesome?

I can look after him, says Jordy.

You're not my babysitter, I say.

You're younger than me.

We're nearly the same age.

Are not.

At the start of the year, we're only a year apart.

So. What.

So.

I see him look at her, then back at me, and swallow what he is going to say.

149

Hey, you're both pretty grown-up. That's pretty excellent, she says and smiles a giant smile at us.

We've got Nev, though, from across the road, I say. I don't know why I say it, and I want to suck the words right back inside me.

She looks at Nev's caravan. Oh, she says, yeah, okay. She shifts the baby on her hip. Comes back to us with a smile. Well, I'll let you kids be, hey. Tell your mum I came by. See ya later. She starts back down the road towards the tents.

Bye, I say with a grin.

Jordy looks at me like I've betrayed something and my grin turns brittle.

You know what happens, he says. They put you in a foster home. We never see each other again, and Loretta goes to jail.

Shut up, I say and get the half-broken chair and perch on it. I'm so thirsty. I lick my dry, cracked lips. My bottom lip feels fat under my tongue. We both look over at Nev's caravan. I can smell the gummy.

It's what happens, he repeats.

I find an old tennis ball in the drawer. I try squish it in my fist but it's still hard. It's grey and bald in spots.

Wanna play catch? I ask.

Yeah, nah, Jordy says.

I throw the ball from hand to hand. Feel its rough fur. I throw it gently at Jordy. He doesn't catch it but lets it land on him and roll off. I get up, grab it, brush the sand off with my fingertips and throw it at him again. He makes no motion to get it, and it rolls away again.

Why are you ignoring me? I say.

I'm not.

I throw the ball at him hard. He doesn't react, just holds the ball after it hits him, and doesn't look at me.

Catch? I say. He doesn't reply, holds on to the ball. I go sit back outside. After ages he comes and sits outside too.

Stop scratching your bites, he says.

I'm not scratching them.

I pull the ball from his hand. I throw it against the side of the caravan and it makes a bang that shakes salt and rust. The ball rolls back towards my feet. I throw it again.

You don't want to play? I say to Jordy. He rolls his eyes and sits down, hunches over his knees. I throw the ball at the caravan. After the noise and the flakes of rust have settled I hear one sharp clap from across the road. I look over my shoulder. Nev is there and he mouths the words, Stop it. Or he says it quietly. I wonder how long he's been standing there, watching. My skin shrinks. I hide behind Jordy. When I look next Nev is gone. I pick up the balding ball in my hand and squeeze. It cracks down the side. Inside it's dirty and smells plastic and strange. I scrunch my nose, throw the ball to the dunes. We wait for the afternoon, and then for night. I couldn't say how many days we've been here, in my mind they've all mixed into one.

The air is still. I can hear conversations all the way from where the tents are. Like the people are real close. Around and into the distance there are spots of torchlight and lanterns coming on, one after another. I hear something and I jump. I see things in the shadows. I swallow and calm my breath.

Jordy?

I can hear him rustling inside and he comes out with the stub of a candle and a VB lighter. He makes us a small patch of light. His eyes look too big and round. In Nev's caravan the fluoros go on and we can see in there perfectly. I can hear the generator. My stomach swims and grumbles. Nev is there in front of a window. He looks out and I wonder what he can see of us. I can see his watery eyes even from here. He shakes his head and I see his lips moving, he's muttering something to himself. He turns away.

I'm thirsty, I say.

Yeah, so? Jordy bangs up the steps and into the caravan and then straight back out again because there's nothing inside, and it's dark. He sits down beside me. I hear a car from ages away. The growl of it on the corrugations.

Is that her?

How should I know?

I dunno. I bite my pointer fingernail and rip at it until it hurts. It tastes like fish-dirt. Up the road, headlights show over the hill and my heart beats fast. But as the car comes down and past us into the camp, I see it's not Bert. The nose is a different shape. The car is white and new and it drives past without slowing down, leaving behind the smell of hot engine.

The crickets are so loud. When there is no more electric blue in the sky Jordy gets the candle and goes with the wavery light into the caravan. I follow like there's a little piece of string connecting us, and I got no choice but to go with the pull of it.

You wanna sleep there? he says, pointing with the candle at Loretta's bed.

No, I say.

Well, I'm gunna sleep there then. But he doesn't go to get

in the bed. I sit on the edge of the bench seat that becomes my bed. A puff of air farts out of it but this time neither of us laugh. He puts the candle down. We look at the double bed at the end of the caravan, the sheets crumpled as if someone just got up.

Okay, he says, and goes and lies in Loretta's bed, smoothing the sheets out first, then climbing on. He lies there with the stained pillow and his arms under his head. Blow out the candle, he says. I blow it out, and the wick smoke curls and stinks. Loretta always licks her fingers and pinches the wick but I'm too scared of burning myself.

Can I come sleep with you? I say.

No.

I get onto the bench and lie there, running my hands over the underside of the table. I can feel things carved into the bottom of the table. I try trace over them with my fingers. Names, I reckon, I feel *Loretta* there, carved into the wood but I can't be sure. There are shadows on the roof, shifting darkness as if there are night clouds up there. There's a whistle from the wind. Rustling so it sounds like there is someone just there, right outside the door. I can tell Jordy's not asleep, his breaths are short and irregular.

I'm scared, Jordy, I whisper and the words snag in my throat like a fish bone.

What? he says.

I'm scared.

I can't hear what you're saying.

Nothing, I say loudly. Nothing. The words echo in the tinny room.

Jordy.

What?

There's someone outside.

Just shut up, he says, shut up.

I hold my breath, but I can hear someone out there.

Jordy.

Look, he says, and bounds out of the bed, and is at the door. He opens it slowly, worried maybe at the last second that he's wrong. I sit up and stare out with him. There's two eyes there. Jordy stumbles back and the door swings shut. He bangs himself on the table.

Shit. It's a dingo, it's a dingo, he says. He laughs and opens the door again. Shoo, he says. The dingo has his snout in the gummy. He's got the gummy, says Jordy. He goes to step towards it and the dingo stares hard at him and growls. Both the dingo and Jordy step back. The dingo pulls the gummy along.

Jordy claps his hands, Shoo. I pull my knees up and hug myself. Hey, he says and steps down closer, stamping. Hey, he says louder. Hey. He's outside now, with the dingo, the screen door screeches closed.

Give it back, he says. I hear a scuffle and the low growl of the dingo. Then the screech of the door and Jordy's back inside, dragging the gummy in with him.

Shit, he says, shit. He's got the tailfin in his hands. Close the door, close the door, he says. I jump up and pull the screen door shut. But I can see the dingo still pacing outside. The screen door is not a real door either, the dingo could just push its snout through the mesh. The gummy's face looks not quite right, bite marks on him. Jordy drops the tail.

Shit. Shit, he says. I stand up. Through the screen door I can see the glow from Nev's caravan, the lights still on. I wonder if he could hear us if we called out? There isn't enough room for Jordy, me and the gummy. I sit back down. Jordy opens the cupboard. He finds an old bit of newspaper and lays it on top of the gummy, tucking the newspaper around it.

There, he says. But its bitten head is staring at me in the dark. He scrunches a bit of newspaper to wipe his hands.

Just go to sleep, he says. He snaps the lock of the screen door into place. I hear the small click of it. Jordy gets back into Loretta's bed. I can still hear things outside. I imagine lots of things out there, and they're worse than a dingo and its growl. For a long time I listen to Jordy's breathing. When his breathing changes and I am sure he's asleep I step over the gummy and climb onto the edge of Loretta's bed. I make sure I'm really far away from him so he doesn't wake. I scrunch up on the edge. The bed smells of Loretta: cigarettes and too-sweet watermelon deodorant.

13

I wake covered in sweat. I dig the sleep out of my eyes. There's a dream still, somewhere at the edges of my brain, slippery as sand. I open my eyes. Jordy's not there. The bed is empty. I've sprawled to the middle where the foam sags. I sit up. I black out for a second, dizzy, until my brain catches up with my head. My mouth is so dry and tastes horrible. I look around for something to drink before I remember we've got nothing. I shuffle off the bed. It creaks and shudders. I fall over the gummy. Kick its flesh.

Sorry, I say and it comes out a hoarse whisper. I clear my throat. Step over the gummy, open the screen door.

Jordy, I say into the hot. A fly goes straight up my nose and I have to snort it out. It drops halfway to the ground then keeps flying.

Jordy?

I jump into my thongs and walk to the toilet. He's not there. I take a piss and even pissing into the dark hole I can tell my piss is brown and gross. I climb to the top of the dune and look out at the beach. It is still and coloured better than jewels. I walk back to the caravan and my head beats with my heart. I look back in there. Jordy? The gummy's broken fin sticks out from under the newspaper. The flies slip in the open door. I turn to look at Nev's caravan and my headache beats faster. I put one foot in front of the other and cross the road. I step in the dips of the corrugations. I count my steps in my mind. It takes thirty-seven steps to reach the back of the caravan. I concentrate on my feet and don't look up. I hear Nev talking to Jordy and I have to.

Please don't come here, he says. Nev runs his hands through his grey hair. It's like torture, he says. He closes his eyes and holds his hand out as if to stop the day moving forward. Standing there on stick, old-person legs. I can see through the skin on his legs. I can see his veins, his insides. Like a ghost crab's shell, he's see-through. Jordy sees me.

We need a drink of water, he says, please.

Nev, hearing the *we*, opens his eyes and looks right at me. I see a tear squeeze out the corner of his eye.

Fuck, he says, and wipes the tear away. You'll ruin me, he says. He goes into the caravan.

Jordy, quick, I say. I grab his arm and he shakes me off.

No, he says.

Nev comes out with two metal cups and a bottle of Coke. He sits down at his camp table that sags in the middle like it's tired. He balances the bottle and the cups there in the centre and pours us a glass each. The coldness beads off them. I look at Jordy and he reaches over and takes a cup. I walk closer and take a cup too, but step quickly back. I don't look at Nev. I sip it and it's so sweet it burns my throat. The bubbles go up my nose and I cough, spitting Coke out onto the ground. It evaporates straight away. I take a deep breath and drink the rest slowly. A butcherbird swoops down and lands on the edge of the caravan windowsill. It taps its beak on the glass. Tap. Tap, says the butcherbird. Tap. It sharpens its beak on the metal edge of the sill then stops, cocks its head and looks at me with one eye.

I look at Nev. He has his head in his hands. I get the vision of him and Jordy come into my head bright as a television screen. I try to shake it out.

Just go, says Nev.

Jordy and I stand there with empty cups.

Get, he says.

But we need some water, Jordy says.

He looks up at us and says, Get. He stands up, flexing his old man muscles.

I drop my cup and run. I stumble and bang against the side of the caravan. It sounds hollow as a drum. I can hear the slap of Jordy's thongs as he walks behind me. My stomach feels gross and strange with the drink in it. I imagine it in there, black. At the road I stop. The woman is there, at the front of our caravan, with a man. She's got the baby on her hip. Jordy bumps into the back of me.

The woman jumps a little when she hears us. Her face looks guilty, like we've caught her at something. She has her hair up in a ponytail like how a little girl would wear it. A blush colours her face all the way down to her chest and shoulders. The man puts his hand on her arm. He looks like all the other men here. A floppy hat over his eyes, and skin made hard and brown by the sun.

Oh hi, she says and changes her face into a happy one, puts on a smile.

Hi, I say – with the gravel road between us. Jordy steps around me. His giant singlet slips off his shoulder and I see the burn the sun has made there. The man is wearing a faded T-shirt. I can make out a date on it, from ten years ago. He lets go of his wife. Holds his hands in front of him, like he's just discovered them and doesn't know what to do.

Hello, he says. His voice is low and slow as a brown river.

I just came to say hi, she says. The little girl on her hip starts to cry. The inside of her mouth is the brightest red.

Loretta's not here, says Jordy.

The woman looks at the man, as if to say, See. I just wanted to – she says and doesn't seem to be able to finish it off. She adjusts her baby, wipes the little girl's sweaty hair from her forehead. Gives her a quick kiss. You know, if you kids need anything, you just gotta ask. I could call someone. We're in the big blue tent, just down there. Her baby takes a giant breath then wails. Sweetie, come on, she says and bounces the baby on her hip. She looks at her husband and he shakes his head.

Nah, we don't need anything, says Jordy but it's hidden under the crying.

Okay, okay, sweetie, she says. She wipes damp hair from her own forehead with the back of her hand. I think she looks really young then, younger than Loretta. She doesn't have much wrinkles in her face when she smiles, not like Gran whose face cracks when she's happy.

The man looks at us, and leans in, says something I can't hear to the woman's ear. She looks angry, cuts him off with a hissed whisper. The baby wails. Okay, I'll see ya later then, she says to us in a too-cheery voice.

The lady finds her husband's hand. They walk away together. She looks back once. Jordy and I are still standing in the sun in the middle of the road.

I can hear a car coming, but it sounds nothing like Bert, it growls loud. I smell the dirt before the car gets there.

Jordy pulls me by the arm, Get off of the road, dumb-ass, he says.

The back of a truck swings out as it turns the corner down to the beachfront. It's got beady bug eye spotties on the roof. As they pass us they slow down and I can see there's two men in the front. The driver leans out his window and yells at us, Happy New Year, throws a can of bourbon. It's badly aimed and lands metres away from us, fizzing. Flies land on the spilled drink straight away. Gravel peppers us as they drive further into the camp and I flinch.

I hope the mum and baby are off the road, I say.

Jordy stoops in under our awning. He sits in the small section of shade. I follow him.

You want to sit a bit closer to me? he says.

I shift further away. A marchfly buzzes with its too-heavy body. I feel the marchy give up and land on my leg. I know if I move now it'll fly away and be back in a minute to get me again. Got to let the marchy bite. I let it bite. Jordy seeing it there leans over and slaps my leg. The marchy falls to the ground and I watch the ants find it in one second.

Don't tell Loretta, he says.

Don't tell Loretta what? I say.

If we find her, don't tell her what happened.

I dig into the sand at my feet. I hear a crow caw. The metallic sound of its claws on the roof of the caravan. It's so quiet I hear its wings settle into place.

What even happened?

Nothing, he says and gives me a look that's hate right the way from his head to his toes.

How are we going to find her?

I'm going to ask him to take us to look for her.

No, I say quietly. I don't want to go with him.

I'm going on my own.

No.

The ants are trying to drag the marchy, but they only manage to pull it a little way. Flies crawl onto me. I swat them away. They can smell the gummy. I taste the sugar in my mouth.

The gummy smells bad, Jordy, I say. I look at him.

I know.

He told us to go away.

Yeah, I know, Tom. But he'll take me.

The wind blows and snaps the awning. For a moment it's cooler than before. I look at him and he looks away. The sun climbs a little bit higher.

What are we going to do?

I'm going to think for a bit, he says.

A while later I see the husband drive past us on the way into town. He raises a finger in greeting. We stare back.

Nosey parker, says Jordy, how Loretta would say it. The car's dust settles on us.

Tom, wake up, Jordy says.

With my eyes closed the world is soft and pink. Jordy shakes me hard. I open my eyes and I can't see anything. It's so bright. My head feels heavy. I close my eyes again. I reach out. Jordy pulls me to my feet.

Get up, he says.

I open my eyes again. He's right there close to my face.

Do what I say, he says and pulls me towards the dunes. Run, he says. Run.

His hand on my arm hurts, but I'm too asleep to tell him to stop. My thongs throw sand up the back of my legs and make a snap, snap sound. I try say something but my mouth is so dry it only comes out a croak. I lick my cracked lips and taste blood. He pushes me over the hump of the first dune and pulls me to the sand.

What? I say.

Shut up, he says.

I close my eyes and feel the thump thump of the headache that's there all the time now. It feels just like the beating of my heart, like if it stopped I'd die. I go to speak again, with my eyes closed still, but he squeezes my arm hard to stop me. I open my eyes and swallow. The sand is burning hot. Jordy commandos up to the top of the dune, flat on his belly. I slither up next to him until we can just see over the top, between the waving grass. Up close the blades of grass have a soft grey fur. I try dig my body into the sand to where it's cool, like I seen a kangaroo do.

Jor– I say but he cuts me off with a low *Shhhhh*.

A police car stops in front of the caravan and idles, shudders off. A young cop doubles in size when he unfolds himself out of the passenger side. He's long and skinny. His gun belt looks too heavy and hangs off his waist. His eyes hidden behind wraparound sunnies. He leans back in the window and says something I can't hear. The other cop gets out too. He's older, with grey hair wisping out from beneath his hat. His gut hangs over his belt, his shirt holding it like a pouch.

Take a look then, eh, says the older one who speaks without opening his mouth. The lines on his face are deep enough to rest a cigarette.

Sure thing, boss, says the tall one. He walks to our caravan, leans in under the awning. He has to stoop. I hold my breath.

It doesn't smell good, he yells back. The other cop lights up, drags on his cigarette and leans back on the car.

Well, take a look, he says.

I hear the screen door open.

Oh Jesus Christ, I hear from the caravan. Fucken hell. Fuck. He laughs nervously. Holy shit, he says.

The other cop takes a long drag on his cigarette before dropping it onto the gravel road. The tall one comes back out from under the awning, shaking his head. He takes his sunnies off, wipes the sweat from his face on his shirtsleeve. They've both got new moons of sweat at their armpits.

So? says the older one. Body?

There's a big dead fish in there.

The old one raises his eyebrows. Really?

Yep.

Well, I'll be damned. He goes has a look for himself.

What are they going to do to it? I whisper.

Shut up.

But what if they take her?

163

Shhh. He punches me in the arm, but he can't get a good angle lying on the ground, so it just feels lame.

I hear the cop cough as he comes back out.

It's a shark, he says, not a fish.

I thought it was going to be my first body, the younger one says.

The old one shrugs his shoulders and they both look around. We flatten ourselves to the ground. I feel their eyes on us in the dunes, but time goes and they must pass over. When I look up again, Jordy has his face in the sand. He looks me in the eye and when he lifts his face, it is half-covered in white sand. The police are at Nev's door. I hear the tinny knock, knock, knock.

Nev walks around the side. He stops when he sees them. I can't hear what they're saying but he talks there with the cops, as if they all know each other. The cops stand in the neat sun. Nev hides in the darkness of the shade.

What are they saying? I whisper to Jordy.

Shh, he says, he won't dob.

Do you reckon they'll take the gummy?

Shut up.

The cops point to our caravan and I see Nev shrug his shoulders. They scan the dunes again. I flatten myself against the sand. Put my face into the heat, scrunching my eyes shut. I realise I'm saying, Please, please, please, please, please over and over again in my head, but I don't know what I'm asking please for.

I hear their car start and it's only when the sound disappears altogether that I dare to look up.

They're gone, stupid, says Jordy. He's sitting up on the sand. I look at him, but I can't see his expression 'cos his face is deep in its own shadow.

We gotta get the gummy outta there, he says.

I can see Nev still standing in the doorway at the front of his caravan. I don't want to move until he's gone. He walks out into the sun, then changes his mind, goes back into his caravan, letting the screen door bang behind him. I sit up, sand all over me.

Come on, Jordy says.

He gets up and I follow him down the dune to the caravan. He opens the door. The stink is bad, it makes my lips curl into a snarl. I look under Jordy's arm. The gummy is in there on the floor. It looks sad and out of place. The newspaper covering is off. There are so many flies.

Jordy goes into our caravan and stands over the gummy.

Help me, he says.

I go in there, but with the three of us, the room is heaps too small. I get the gummy's head in my hands. It slips out and slams on the lino. My hands are covered in sandy slime. Liquid oozes out of the head.

Come on, useless, he says.

I grab it again, holding tight this time. Jordy's got the tail gripped in his hands. He backs out of the screen door. The flies crawl all over me and I can't let go to shoo them off. I shake my head and try to shake them from my nose and around my eyes. We hold it with its belly sagging between us and stumble out the door into the sun.

Where should we put her? I say.

I don't know, he says quietly.

I hear another car. We look at each other, a little whimper escapes my mouth.

Quick, says Jordy. He pulls away from me and I nearly lose grip on the gummy. My fingers dig into its mouth, touch its sharp little teeth.

We cross the road towards Nev's truck. It's nudged in against his caravan, with the tray towards us. The glare off the white stings my eyes and I wonder where my sunglasses are, if Loretta took them with her in Bert.

Here, says Jordy.

He lifts the gummy up and over the edge of the truck, into the tray. It flops in there, stinking, with a bang.

Shit, he says.

We crouch down next to the wheel. My heart beating as fast as my headache. Nev doesn't come, though, and the car passes. Not the police. We stand up. I look in the tray at the gummy. I see its cloudy eye looking back at me. A fly lands on its eyeball and I look away.

We should have left it on the beach.

It's our shark, Jordy says.

I lean as far as I can into the tray and grab a scungy towel that's there. I throw it over the gummy. The towel's got oil on it, and grot, but under the dirt is a faded pattern of sailboats. The gummy's tail sticks out, but most of it is covered. The sun's right full on the truck.

Jordy runs his hand along the side of the truck, leaving a long clean line in the dirt. He goes to the side of the caravan and rests his hand there.

I grab his shirt and say, Jordy. But he shrugs me off. He goes and peeks around the edge and I follow him because I've got no other choice.

Out the back I can see the dirt separated from the other

dirt by the white border of rocks. Nev's up on a wobbly plastic chair. He's got one of the whirling glass globes in his hand. Cradled by rope, he unhooks it from the caravan roof. It hangs from his arm. He looks unsure of what to do next, leans down and gets off the chair. He sits on the chair and the globe rests in his lap like a cloudy crystal ball. The other buoys have been taken down too. They're in the dirt. There's a crate at his feet, full of fishing equipment, reels and a net poking out. In another crate there's plates and mugs, kitchen things that he's cleared out of the caravan. He's packing everything up. He has a beer beside him. He takes a big gulp, crunches the can and throws it into the bush. The generator clicks on. The sound of it vibrates in my head. I lean on Jordy, pull on his singlet. He comes with me then. We're standing out on the gravel road and I can't do anything but lead him back to our caravan. Looking inside the caravan there is sand on the floor and the smell of the gummy lingers.

I can't do it, he says.

What?

I can't just sit here.

I don't say nothing.

You stay here, wait for me, says Jordy.

No way.

I'll be back, I promise.

Don't leave me.

But it's safer.

It's not safer, Jordy. That's bullshit.

His face screws up.

You can't leave me here, I say.

I'm not leaving you, I'm just going to go find her.

I grab a hold of his singlet and twist it around my fingers. He pulls away and it makes a little ripping sound.

Let go.

No.

Let go, Tom, he says and slaps me roughly but not hard on the side of my head.

No.

He tries to grab me, but the singlet rips a little more.

Okay, he hisses, Jesus.

I let go of the fabric. It's pulled out of shape at one corner. He tries to even it up, pulls the other side.

Well, come on then, he says. And walks back over the road and around to the back of the caravan. Nev is throwing another empty into the bushes at the back. He spins around when he hears us. All his belongings are messed around his feet, boxes with open tongues. There are tools laid out and looking sharp on the ground.

So? he says.

You have to help us, says Jordy.

No, I don't, he says.

The police were here, says Jordy.

I know they were bloody well here.

We need to look for Loretta.

Listen, son, he says.

I'm not your son, says Jordy.

He sighs and looks to the sky.

I'm not taking you anywhere.

You have to.

Son, no, I don't. You got nothing to offer.

I could tell them.

I feel Jordy square his shoulders beside me. I want to cry.

Tell them what, son? He picks a spade up off the ground and leans on it. I'm leaving anyway, he says. It don't matter. You think she's out there?

She was last time, he says.

You two are poor excuses, Nev says. But he looks away when he says this. He drags the spade behind him, and opens another beer from a sixpack that's sweating on the table.

Well, if it'll get rid of you, I'll take you, Nev says. He picks up the rest of the sixpack. He drags the spade with him, around the side. We follow quietly, unsure. He throws the spade in the back of the truck without looking.

Get in the car. Before I change my mind, Nev says. Our shadows reach their long limbs towards him.

Jordy, I don't want to go with him, I whisper.

Nev gets in the truck. He twirls his keys in his hands catching them at the end of each twirl, just like last time. But he looks shaky as he climbs into the cab, pulling himself up in there. I can see his face watching us in the mirror. A crow lands on the back of the truck. Nev turns the engine over and revs it.

Stay here then, Jordy says.

No, I say.

I can see Nev's arm hanging out of the cab, a cigarette burning at the end of it. I get up and cross the gravel. I go to open the passenger door. The handle burns me, it's so hot from the sun. Nev puts those sunglasses on his face that have those side bits to keep out every bit of light. Looks at me with them black squares. I try the handle again and this time quickly click it open, so I don't hold it long enough for it burn my palm. Nev's got his ciggie hanging from his bottom lip. Jordy grabs my arm and goes, You should stay. I try pull my arm from his grip but it's a vice.

Get off me, I say.

I'm pulling so hard I sprawl onto the floor of the truck. Empty beer cans clang together and I crunch down on them. Nev's spotty leg is beside me, it's almost hairless, like a lady's. I get up onto the seat. He rips a beer out and cracks it open. He throws the others to the ground and they touch my legs. The cold makes me jump, but then I lean my leg back on them and let the cool get me.

Do you have any water? I say. He nods to the floor of the cab, in among all the empty beer cans is a big juice bottle of water.

Radiator water, he says.

The plastic looks yellow but I reach down and grab it. The bottle is hot. I take a swig and it pours around my mouth and onto my chest. I pass the water to Jordy who has slipped in beside us.

Where are you taking us? I say.

We'll go check for her, he says. Takes a long swig of beer.

I look out at the straight line of the horizon and imagine it joining around behind me, round and tight as a belt. I look at Jordy's hands in his lap and all his fingernails are bitten to nothing. I wonder how I've not noticed him ripping them to pieces. My nails are long, ragged and bright with half circles of lobster-red dirt. Nev pushes a cassette into the tape deck and country music warbles out at us. He bangs my leg with the gear stick, reverses and accelerates too fast out of there. I shrink away from him, but Jordy shrugs me back.

Jordy, I say. He looks at me from beneath his fringe and I

shrink back against him, and he lets me. Nev flicks his butt out the window and starts rolling a ciggie, holding the wheel steady with his knee. The air is a hot, heavy wool blanket. Nev leans forward, cups the ciggie in his hands, lights it.

So, what's with them tattoos anyways? I say. He turns the black squares of his sunglasses on me again.

My kids, he says. They'd be all grown up now. I wouldn't know.

I shrink away.

Hell, I'm probably a grandfather. He laughs but the laugh sounds bad and after a while it turns into a deep racking cough. He spits a huge golly out the window. Sucks his cigarette down. He doesn't say anything more. We all sit there.

At the turn off to the highway I see the yellow of a beat-up car and I catch my heart in my throat, 'cos it looks like the yellow of Bert. A yellow, brown and bubbled with rust. I almost laugh to think she's only made it this far. But as we get closer I can see there are teenage boys standing around the car, and there are surfboards on the roof and there are stickers all over it. As we pass I still expect to see her. I look through the window, but she ain't there drumming her fingers against the steering wheel. The front seat of their car is empty.

One of the boys looks at me. He's got one of them party blowers, like a whistle with a paper tongue, and he blows it at us as we pass. The multicoloured tongue pokes out and curls back. I remember it's New Year's. We turn off the gravel onto the black lick of road.

14

A rock flicks up at the windscreen. It makes a sharp sound. Nev looks in the rear-view mirror for a culprit. The road shimmers with heat. The windscreen has a spiderweb crack.

The crack'll travel. It'll travel, break the window in two by the end, says Nev.

Up ahead I see the Shell sign of the servo. Nev parks the truck in the shade cast by the building. I can't see Bert. There's two girls filling their Kombi at the pumps. They look like overgrown kids, unwashed, with tumbled hair and sleepy eyes. Written in the dust on their back windscreen is *wash me*.

I'll go ask, says Jordy and clicks the car door open. I look over at Nev who's lighting another ciggie, and I jump out too. But before I go I say, You're not supposed to smoke at a service station.

He raises his eyebrows at me and taps his ash out the window.

I can see Jordy through the glass of the servo door, leaning over the counter, talking to the girl. I don't follow Jordy in, but instead walk around the side of the building. Near the bins, there's a huge cage with a cockatoo bobbing its head at me. Hello dicky, hello dicky, it says. Then it makes the clicking sounds just like the pump does when the fuel tank's full. Click, click, click. I click my tongue back at it.

Hello dicky, hello dicky, the cockatoo bounces his head. A sign written in Texta says, *Look out. He bites.* Bounce, bounce, behind the cage. I put my finger through the wire to see. The cocky lunges towards me and I pull my finger out of there quick as. Hello, I say to it. You do bite, eh. It looks at me, then nibbles a hanging seed bell, cracking seeds and dropping them to the littered cage floor.

Some chickens peck at red dirt outside a dark doorway into the back of the roadhouse. Their bellies must be full of dirt. I rub my eyes hard, try to see as I step into the shade of the doorway. Look inside. There's a Christmas tree in the corner. Its lights going flicker, flicker, flicker, red, orange, green. There's tinsel strung around it, and a couple of string baubles. The flickery lights light up framed pictures of a man holding a barramundi, and his own grin. Old wedding photos, black-and-white but coloured-in with faded pastel. There's a picture of a kid with a footy under his arm. A breeze blows a row of Christmas cards to the ground. I go try to pick them up. I put one back and it blows straight off. I look around behind me to see if anyone is watching. I try stand the card back up but I can't get it right. It's got a kangaroo on a surfboard dressed like Santa. I let it drop to the floor.

An old woman is at the door. She's wrinkly as a prune. Her

173

dress floats around her. She sees me, shuffles forward and smiles a toothless smile. She's so thin. I say, Hello. She taps her ear with a gnarly finger and shakes her head. She shuffles back out again. She comes back with fruitcake. Her turkey-wattle arms wobble. She smiles at me again.

She looks at me, and a voice booms out of her little frame, slurred, all the words swarming together into one. I-can't-hear-love, she says.

She gives me a plate with roses all linked up around the edges of it. It makes me thirsty just looking at it, it looks so dry. She motions for me to eat it. My hand is shaking when I reach to take a bite. Crumbs fall from me. She leans back, crosses her arms to watch. It takes me a really long time to chew it and swallow. It's made cement in my mouth. Can I've a drink? I say and make a drinking motion. Please. But it's like she can't see or hear me now, and she don't get me nothing. I step back slowly. I trip on a pile of old newspapers and the plate crashes to the ground. Miraculously it don't break, but I make a run for it. The square of the door shines bright.

Back outside I can see a long shed, it's shiny new. There are other sheds past it, each one more crumbled down and rusty than the last. On the horizon I can see the shadowy smudge of a ridge. I kick over a rusty old tin of cigarette butts and it makes a hollow gong. It spills the butts out. I look around, right the tin and leave the butts there. I walk the long way around the buildings back to the front. There is an orange phone booth. It stands out by the road, strange and separate from anything. For a second I think Nev has left me behind, but he's just moved the ute.

Down the road, a guy walks out of the mirage. The black snakey line of him forms into a person. He flings the roadhouse door open. I follow him in. He goes to the fridge and gets out a long cold bottle of water and buys it with coins he magics from the pocket of his overalls. Up close his skin is like leather. He pays the girl, who isn't as pretty as the one that was here last time, but has freckles across her nose and cheeks that look like they're drawn on with a brown crayon, which I like.

Hey, I say to him when he turns around. He looks at me, startled, and grunts what I reckon is a hello, and starts walking.

Hey, I go again, can I ask you a question?

He stops and looks down at me, scratches the stubble on his face.

Did you see a yellow car drive past today or yesterday? I say.

A yellow car? he says and scratches first the side of his face, then behind his ears, then across his chest. It's as if with the scratch he's sifting through all the memories. I hold my breath. Goosebumps on my arms from the air-con.

No, he says. I ain't seen a yellow car today.

He sits himself down at one of them plastic tables, and I'm standing stranded there in the middle of the floor. I search around to rest my hands on something. I have to walk to the counter to lean against it.

What can I get you? says the girl with the freckle nose – and this one has an English accent straight off the ABC. Are you alright? she asks.

I see Jordy walking towards me from the toilets, and I say to her, Yep, I'm okay. I let go of the counter.

She reckons she ain't seen Loretta, he goes. But she only come on at lunch, and the owners have gone into town 'cos it's New Year's. What were you talkin' to him for? Jordy goes.

I don't know. We step back out into the heat.

Look. Jordy points to the tap sticking out of a cement square. I laugh. He turns it on and I stick my head right the way under there and let the water run into my mouth. It tastes metallic and the first bit is so hot I flinch. But then it's cool. Jordy pushes me out of the way and I choke, spluttering beside him. I watch his hair go slick and see his eyes closed tight. I look to the ute and pull Jordy from the tap. We walk back.

Hello dicky, I whisper to myself, Hello dicky, hello dicky, hello dicky. Walking past the phone booth I push open the door and check the change slot for coins. But inside it's smooth and empty. Hello dicky, I say, hello dicky, wondering who the cocky's mimicking. The crows are circling us from above.

I can't see Nev in the truck. When we come around the side of the tray he's standing there, looking out towards the desert. He jumps when I say, Hey.

But then he says, Have ya ever hypnotised a chicken? He's got a beer. He takes a long swig of the can, empties it, crunches the can and pots it into the back of the truck. There is a chicken lying in front of him. Its wings are splayed out, white wings gone orange with dirt. Its little beaky head is turned to the side. It looks dead.

No, I say.

When he touches it, it springs back to life. It clucks and flaps its feathers, remembering they're there. Its eyes are shiny as beads. He pushes the chook's head back into the dirt. He traces a line back and forth in front of the chook's beak, drawing a line in the dust. The chicken stills. Everything is still. Nev stands, lights a new cigarette. He blows smoke signals into the sky.

If you put a hat over a sheep's head, it'll lay there forever, terrified of the dark, he says.

What's that supposed to mean? says Jordy.

Nev grins and shrugs. I wonder if the chicken might lie there until it starves to death, or the ants find it. Nev claps his hands and the chicken squawks up alive and screaming. It zigzags away from the roadhouse and into the scrub like it's being pursued.

Nev drops his cigarette butt, gets back into the truck and starts it up. The exhaust smells sweet blowing back at us. The stub of his cigarette is the colour and shape of a child's severed finger. In the dust I can see the flat shape where the chicken was lying dead.

What should we do, Jordy?

I don't know. Get in the car.

I'm still thirsty.

Yeah.

The water has dried on us already. I can smell the gummy. Three crows sit on the edge of the tray. They caw. Show me inside their beaks.

Get lost, Jordy tells them. They turn their heads and put us in the sights of one of their eyes but don't move. Jordy opens the door. Nev's finishing another can of beer. He throws it on the floor. It tinkles like Christmas. I climb up in there. Jordy follows.

We'll check in town, he says. Reverses and pulls out onto the highway with a shower of gravel. The crows are in the rear-view mirror, still on the back of the tray. When we go fast enough they fly up. I close my eyes. Watch the world go dark rosy red. I look at the inside of my eyelids.

Loretta leans down to kiss the top of my head. Her hair brushes my face, it tickles and I laugh. I can smell watermelon.

Boy, you've grown tall, she says and laughs. She brushes her hair behind her ears and stands back to look at me. See my dress, it's new, she says. She holds her dress out for me, and she looks beautiful. She twirls around and around and then stumbles. Dizzy, she says and laughs again. What about you? You good?

I gasp. Open my eyes. The road is rushing towards me. I try sit up straight, brace myself. My legs are stuck to the seat with sweat. I wake up properly and remember we're just driving.

Here, I stole this, says Jordy. He opens my hand and puts a Redskin in it. I tried to get a drink but the girl was watching.

I look at the lolly. My mouth feels like the bottom of a birdcage. I think of Loretta.

Thanks, I say. Close my fingers over it.

It's cool, says Jordy. I look up at him and his mouth is full of red. I cringe away from him, touch Nev, cringe away. I try to keep in the middle. I want to tell Jordy my dream, but I don't want Nev to hear. It's slipping away anyway. I can only remember her face as she stumbled.

Shit, willy-willy, says Nev. There's a twisting black curl coming towards us. Burnt earth, rocks, and sticks as high as the sky. It looks strong enough to catch birds. He slows the car.

What's a willy-willy? I say.

It's a pain, is what it is. Wind your windows up, he says.

Nev opens a new beer. The can cracks and sprays warm beer on me. He takes a swig then wedges the can between his thighs. The willy-willy heads for us. He swings the truck onto the side of the road. Brush scrapes at the underside of the car. The sound of little branches on metal makes my teeth grind together. The truck stops. There is a beading line of sweat on Nev's upper lip and beer spilt on his thighs. The willy-willy is pulling all the dust from the earth into a cloud. Jordy does up his window and Nev does too. Rocks clatter against the truck and it's darker and red outside. The sticks make a bigger bang. The ignition cuts.

Should we be scared? says Jordy.

Nev laughs. Swigs his beer.

I dig my fingers into the fraying holes in the seat. I feel an inner spring. It's too hot with the windows up. I try breathe slowly. Bits of the door are rusted through. Little whirls of dust spiral into the truck. I see outside, the shine of rubbish – the inside of a chip packet or chocolate bar wrapper. All the hairs on my arms are standing on their ends. Nev winces as sticks hit the truck. He doesn't notice the beer can drop from in between his legs to the floor where it pools around our feet. I hold my breath. I start counting. If I get to one hundred and it still hasn't stopped I'm getting out. Nev sits back and puts his arm up and around mine and Jordy's shoulders. I feel the pressure of his arm at the back of my head. I can smell his underarms, cigarettes and booze. I lean over Jordy and open the door. The wind catches it, pulls it open. Sucks out rubbish and empty beer cans from the car floor. Pulls all my hair in the one direction.

Tom, screams Jordy and tries to close the door, but his hands come up with nothing.

I climb over him and fall out. I sprawl on the ground. I keep my eyes closed tight. Little rocks pepper my skin. Nev is hollering from the truck but it sounds far away. I hear the car door slam shut with me left outside. Beneath it all I feel a strangeness in my stomach. I shouldn't leave them alone. But

I can't do anything except make myself into a ball. The wind comes at me from all directions.

Then it's quiet. I open my eyes and unclench my hands. On the ground there's no leaves or nothing. It's all been sucked up. The ground is smooth. Looking at my arms I see little nicks all over my skin, dots of blood. I rub my eyes, get up. My legs are jelly and it feels funny to be standing. I run my hand over the little silver dints in the paintwork. Jordy looks out at me through the glass. I look away, scratch at my scabbing arms. I hear a door slam and Nev is out of his side. He comes around to look at me.

You stupid or something? he says to me.

No, I say.

He runs his hands through what's left of his hair. Leans on the truck.

Leave him alone, says Jordy, and he's out of the truck now too.

I'm tired, Nev says. He shake his head at us.

Light glares between us all. Nev goes for the spade in the tray. I smell something rotten and for a moment I can't think what it could be.

What's this then? he says.

Nothing, says Jordy.

Jordy looks in the back too and from his face I see we're in trouble. I curl my neck over the edge of the tray. The rotten towel is gone. The gummy looks hard but it smells soft. There are flies all over it.

I said, what's this then, eh?

We didn't want to leave it, says Jordy.

Leave it where?

On the beach, Jordy says quietly, like he knows it sounds dumb.

The gummy looks at me with its eye. I can see the wound where the hook went in, puckered and full of fly.

You didn't even gut it or nothin? says Nev. He reaches in to grab the tail, but his hand slips with the sliminess. Fuck, he says.

No, I say.

Jordy says it too, No.

Nev goes to grab it again.

We're carryin' it with us, I say. We can't leave it out here.

Bullshit, says Nev. Get in there. You're pullin' it out.

We can't leave it here, says Jordy.

We leave it here, or I leave you here with it.

I don't believe you.

Nev shrugs, wipes his hands on his shorts. Try me, he says.

He takes his tobacco out and rolls a cigarette. I look at the sky. The crows have followed us. Black scraps of them against the blue. Nev makes his tongue pointy and licks along the line of his paper. I shudder. He rolls it, lights it, goes to the back of the tray and pulls out the rusty metal bits that hold the back flap up. He folds down the back flap. The spade and the gummy are all that's in there. Nev gets the spade, drags it out of there.

Go on, says Nev. Get it out.

Jordy looks at me, then says, Okay.

Whatever, I don't care, I say.

Jordy climbs up. He looks tall. I hook my fingers over the edge and lean in. He hugs the gummy. He tries to lift it but it slips from his hands. Jordy looks at me like it's my fault and reaches down again. He gets it. It looks liquid. Its head hangs over his arms. It's about as big as a child. He walks with it to the edge of the tray and pauses. The crows fly lower.

Tom, he says.

What.

Help me.

I stand beneath him.

Hold your arms out, he says. I put my arms out, palms up. The gummy half slips, half drops from his hands. It thuds into me and its belly splits open. But I hold it. There is mess smeared all over Jordy's singlet. Jordy jumps down beside me. Guts drip from my arms. They're coloured bright purple and orange. If they didn't smell so bad, they'd be pretty. I gag.

Bury it, says Nev and throws the spade at Jordy's feet.

Why'd you bring that spade anyway? says Jordy.

He smirks at us and I don't know why we thought he could ever help. He finishes his cigarette and starts rolling another, ignoring us. The crows land close. They caw.

Come on, says Jordy. He holds the tail like you hold a hand and we walk away together. He drags the spade behind him.

Okay, he says. Drops the spade. I try not to drop the gummy, but I do. Against the red dirt, its skin is the colour of stormy sky. I wipe the grot from the front of my shirt. It smears it worse and there's nowhere to wipe my hands. I look back at Nev and he's facing the other direction, not even watching us. The crows are, though. They're on the ground hopping towards us. Hop, hop. Not even a flutter of their wings. They stop when I look at them. But when I look back next they're closer.

We could run, I say.

Where? Out there? Jordy says. He gets the spade and starts digging.

I can help, I say.

You're too small.

He makes a hole with a clumpy pile of red dirt beside it. His singlet becomes wet with sweat. When the hole looks about big enough to fit me in it he stops. He gets the old rusty caravan knife out from his pocket.

What are you doing? I say.

I want to keep something, he says.

He leans down and slices into the mouth of the gummy.

Jordy, I say.

What?

Nothing, I guess, I say.

I watch him clamp his hands on the head, his knee on the body, as he cuts the jaw out. Pink tendons cling to it and when it finally comes free the teeth have a grey and red edge of gross lips. I touch all the layered little teeth. A breeze blows the stench away for a second. I give the gummy a little pat on its rough back.

Sorry, I say to it.

When I look at Jordy he's crying. His tears are silent, slow and fat. They leave clean tracks down his cheeks. I start to cry too. He holds the teeth in his hand.

Okay, says Jordy. Wiping tears and snot on his already muck-covered singlet. Let's roll it in, he says.

We get our hands under it. It rolls into the grave, but the hole's too small. The tailfin pokes above the ground. The ants have found us. A line of them has made a road towards us. They crawl all over the gummy.

Nev casts us into shadow. Finished? he says. I step as far away from him as I can, behind Jordy.

Yeah, says Jordy.

The gummy's belly is cream-coloured where it's not split. Jordy starts clomping the dirt back onto it. The grey skin gets half covered over. The tail still out. Jordy drops the spade. He picks up the gummy's teeth. It's black with ants. He shakes them off, but I see them crawling up his arm.

Well, hurry up then, says Nev and he walks back to the truck. We follow him. When I look back the crows have the tail in their beaks and they're pulling.

Come on, Jordy says.

But – I say.

Come on.

He pulls me back towards the truck and the road that's gone liquid in the heat. Nev revs and revs and part of me wishes he'd drive off without us. But we get back in the truck.

The smell of rotting gummy is all over us. I look down at my lap, my palms like two slabs of pink meat. I feel something tickly around my feet. There's ants all over me. I try and get them off, but I can't do it without killing them. There's that crushed ant smell. It reminds me of death. More than maggots, it's ants. I squish them ants one by one.

I'm thirsty, I say.

Nev throws a beer can in my lap. I roll it in between my hands. It's warm. I crack it open and it hisses at me and over-flows onto my legs.

Tom, no, says Jordy. Nev laughs at him, grabs it out of my hands, spilling more on me. He takes a long swig of it, then throws it out the window.

I dig at the holes in the seat with my fingers again. Through the windscreen I see the glint of a chip packet as it falls from the sky, slow as a feather.

Where are we going? I say.

Town, says Nev.

15

The car engine tick tick ticks. The truck is nudged up to the pub. The sun has bleached the colour from everything.

I'm getting a beer, says Nev.

He opens the door and swings himself out. Jordy gets out too. I try get out but the dirty seatbelt holds me. Jordy looks back at me. His singlet is covered in guts. I unclick my belt, slide out.

Jordy has the gummy's jaw in his hands. He looks at it like he doesn't know whether to leave it in the car, but then shakes his head, walks towards the pub door. I walk into the pub, following Jordy, and it's black. I can't see nothing. My eyes come right and Nev's there pulling me in, his hand at the back of my neck, You're alright, son. You're alright.

You're hurting me.

Bullshit, he says and releases my neck to slap me hard on the back.

Everyone is looking at us. I smooth down the goosebumps on my arm. It feels cold in here. The men's arses hang over the bar stools. The old men have creviced faces. Some of them have tattoos right up their legs.

Come on, he says and pushes Jordy and me towards the bar. Sit there, he says. I climb up onto a stool. I bang my feet against the bar. Jordy slides onto the stool next to me.

The lady behind the counter leans over the bar and her breasts squish together. The skin there is wrinkly and slack. It looks like old man's bum crack.

How hot is it? she says as hello.

I don't answer. Behind her is a faded photo of a machine with a wheel as big as a house. There is a little man standing next to it. Next to the picture there is a shark's jaw mounted above the bar with its rows of teeth. It's a big jaw. It would fit me and Jordy in it.

A beer, love, Nev says, and two Cokes.

She stares at us a little while longer, but shrugs, gets his beer. I can feel the boy tattoo looking at me from Nev's arm. He's hanging his head over his beer now, deflated, like that's all that's in him, that sentence, and now he's spoken it there's nothing to hold him up. I can hear two old men laughing. The laughs turn into coughs. I look over at them and they're heaving and spluttering at the table. A basket of potato chips untouched between them. Jordy pushes his stool back and it makes a scraping sound that crawls my skin.

Jordy? I say.

He rolls his eyes at me. I'm going to the toilet.

The lady behind the bar throws a coaster in front of me and places a Coke with ice on it. It's cool and clean. I take a long sip. The sugar rushes at me. I almost laugh. She leans over the counter at me again. Her arms are crossed in a fleshy bow. I look up at her face. Her eyes are brown with chips of blue-green, a colour as strange as an opal. Pretty. I can't look away. Looking into them eyes is like staring at the edge of a shimmering universe.

What are you kids up to? she says.

Nothing.

What you doing with old codger then, eh?

Nothing, I say again and look away from her shimmery eyes, drink my Coke all in one long gulp 'cos I don't know when we're going to have to leave.

Love, says one of the young guys down the line, beer?

All their heads are turned towards us. She puts her hand under my chin and makes me look up at her.

Give me a look at ya, she says.

She shakes her head and leaves me there on the stool. I get the ice and crunch the pieces one by one in my mouth. The sound is loud. When Jordy hasn't come back by the time I have crunched all the ice I get up and go find him.

My feet stick to the carpet. I pass little tables with doily tablecloths and vases with plastic flowers in them. Mosquitoes bump against the fly screens in the back room of the pub. You can see them searching for a hole in the wire. The louvres are open to catch the sea breeze. I go into the Men's.

I lean over. I can see Jordy's thongs and his dirty feet at the gap in the stall. I stand and piss into the trough, aim at the urine cake.

Done a poo yet?

Shut up, says Jordy. My piss splatters up onto my feet. Wet spots in the dust on them. The mosquitoes bump against the wire.

When are we going to look for Loretta?

We are looking for her, he says.

I leave him there. Go hook my fingers over a louvre that's white with dust. There's a chicken out there. I see it pecking around a half-buried beer can. I open the back door of the pub. Step down the cement steps. Mosquitoes swarm to me. The chicken looks at me. It doesn't run, just drags one claw in the dirt. I hold it. My hands on the dusty feathers. I hold it around its neck, which is thin and hard as beef jerky. I push its beak to the side and into the dirt. It's stopped struggling. I draw a line in the dirt in front of its face. Over and over again. Digging my finger in deep. I can feel the heat of the earth through my thongs.

I lift my hand from its neck. It stays there, frozen. I pat its feathers gently and they're slippery. I stand up. The ground is littered with bottle caps, shining their round eyes at me. I dig at one, dislodging it from the earth. I slap a mosquito and it's a bloody splat on my arm. The chicken stays still. I walk backwards up onto the step. Fumble with the door handle and open it. Get in there, back in the cool. The carpet feels spongy under my feet. I look out through the louvres. I can see ants around the chicken already. They've found it. A little cry escapes my mouth. I push open the back door and in the bright sun I clap loudly.

I'm sorry, I'm sorry, I'm sorry, I'm sorry, I'm sorry, I say.

The chicken gets up. Opens its wings and flutters there on the ground, then runs.

I rush past the island tables back to the bar, climb back up the barstool next to Nev. The lady comes back to look at me.

May I have a glass of water, please? I say politely, how Gran would like me to say.

Water, she says, water's for washing the truck. She laughs but gets me a glass. I take a long sip, but leave some for Jordy. It tastes of chlorine. She shakes her head at me, then narrows her eyes at Nev.

These your grandkids?

He looks at her over the top of his beer. Nup.

Well, whose kids are they? she says, but they're talking like I'm not here. I look around and everyone is looking away now, into their laps, their beers, their baskets of chips.

He shrugs. I'm looking after them, he says.

Where they from?

East.

She leans right the way over the bar towards him. Where's their parents?

It ain't your business.

In my pub it's my business.

He shrugs again.

She turns her opal eyes on me, her wrinkles spread across her face into some sort of smile.

Where's your mum and dad? she says.

Nowhere, I say.

Nowhere, she repeats and blows a humph of air out. She steps back and polishes a glass with a tea towel.

Jordy walks towards us over the clear expanse of the room. It feels like it takes him a long time to get to the bar. His eyes look red.

Well, they smell like shit, she says to Nev, gesturing towards us.

I can hear you, I say. She looks like I've slapped her.

Nev eyes her down and scrapes his stool back. Come on, boys, he says.

You give them back, alright, she says. She's cleaning that same glass, twisting it around and around in her hands.

There's no need to worry, he says. These words come out of his mouth so clearly and formally I wonder for a second what he did before he ended up here, at the end of his life. Boys, he says.

I look at her eyes, but she's got them trained on him, and her mouth is pursed tight. I get off my stool and pull on Jordy's singlet.

The men in the pub are still looking into their laps. Nev ushers us towards the door. It swings open. It's blinding out there. I remember my half-glass of water on the bar, the thought is a punch in my guts. I try go back in but Nev has his hand on my neck leading me to the truck.

I make my hands into binoculars. Keep out the glare so that I got two round circles of vision. I look around for Loretta. I put the glittery tar in the circles. I put the takeaway shop in the circles. I try to imagine Loretta in one of the circles, but it's like I've forgotten what she looks like. There's the shuffle, shuffle of Nev's and Jordy's feet. I imagine they're Loretta's feet, I try find them with my binoculars, her toes with the chip of red nail polish in the centre of each nail. The feet that come into the sights are flat and huge. They're Nev's feet. I let the binoculars go and look up at Jordy and him.

Get in the truck, he says.

But what about Loretta? I say.

She ain't here.

But we didn't even ask.

Did it look like she was in there to you?

He goes around to his side, gets in – the keys still hanging from the ignition – doesn't look at us, just looks straight ahead.

Get in, says Jordy. I look at him and he throws his fringe from his face.

Okay, I say, because I don't know what else to do. I take a look down the street before I get in and it's empty. A long stretch of telegraph poles cast lines on the road. I climb back up and it feels like it's the thousandth time I've climbed into the cab.

Nev kicks the engine over and then we sit there, waiting while he rolls a ciggie. He's got that flap of white paper on his lower lip like a bit of flaky skin. I fight the urge to tear it off. He drops the car into gear and reverses out into the street without looking. He has to hold the steering wheel in bursts 'cos of how hot it is. I see two dogs lying in a slip of shade, tongues lolling out of their mouths. I close my eyes and try to forget where I am. I shake my head and whimper without meaning to. Nev changes gears, and I can hear us all breathing. As we drive out of town, I turn around and look back at the Welcome sign and wish we were driving the other way and we could begin again.

Stop squirming, Nev says. I turn back around and sit straight with my hands flat on my sunburnt knees. I scratch my arms. It feels like we're driving straight into the sky. Looking out the front windscreen the road comes up to meet me. The new crack has a tail the length of my pinkie, catching the light. It's been growing. We are driving right into the setting sun. It lights us up golden. The truck visors are down casting little squares of shade on our faces. In the rear-view I can see a few pink clouds. Nev is going fast. We come up on a truck, and there's kids and a mum, and a dad or an uncle holding on tight in the back. They are all smiling. The mum's hair is blowing like a flag and as we pass they all turn to us and blow party tooters. One kid leans over and pops a party popper at us. It bangs. The sun lights up their hair and each of them looks like they got a halo. I gasp. The man driving lifts a hand in greeting. I wave at him, automatically. A beetle smacks against the glass. We've got nothing in the back of our truck.

Nev looks at the two of us and says, Ya know, we were way out deep once, and we come across this white line in the water, looked like a slipstream in the sky and it went as far as I could see from one edge of the ocean to the other. When we got close I realised it was a rope. We pulled it in. It was three thousand metres long and weighed over a ton. I admire something like that, such a long piece of rope. It took up the whole bloody deck. We knotted it into a kind of clumped net and dragged it behind the boat. After a while birds started to alight there. They started nesting there. They picked seaweed out of the water and other bits of flotsam. They laid their eggs right there in the middle of the ocean. The rope got harder and harder to tow, heavier with all the bird shit. Finally we couldn't even pull it. We realised we'd been towing an island, so we cut ourselves free from it.

Jordy sighs and looks at him. What's that supposed to mean?

It means, let it go, he says.

Let what go? I say.

Nev looks at us. You're chasing a mirage.

What?

You don't stand a chance.

I look at Jordy. He looks like he's about to cry. Nev adjusts himself in the seat and shakes his head. I look up at him. He's got grey hair spiralling out of his ears. He grips the steering wheel, accelerating down the road. Jordy scrunches against his door and hangs his arm out the window, palm out, like he's trying to shake hands with the wind. As we turn off tar onto the corrugations the radio fades all the way to fuzz.

16

We drive into the camp. A man staggers across the road in front of the truck. Nev swerves around him. He swerves close to the tents. I look back at the man and he's holding his hand up. Like it's a stop sign. He staggers against the bright blue of dusk. I hear screams of kids playing down the beach. Standing at the crest of a dune a girl is illuminated against the ocean. She collapses suddenly, like she's been shot. But I can hear her giggling maniacally.

I realise I'm holding my breath. I try to force myself to breathe out and in again. My chest hurts. I want to close my eyes but I can't. I count my breaths. The caravans are lit up blue and red. It's like Christmas lights all over again, flashing on and off. Loretta's beach towel is there. Same as this morning. It flaps in the wind. I can see an empty milk arrowroot packet in the grass. Bert's not there. A cop car is shedding light over every-thing. But I can't see any cops.

Get down, says Nev.

Huh? I say.

Get down.

Nev pushes me hard on the shoulder. I crouch down on the floor so as not to touch him, and Jordy's scrunched over the top of me. The empty beer cans collapse under me and leak their hot beer smell.

This is not good, this is not good, he's saying to himself. The corrugations jolt me hard. I bite my cheek. Taste blood. I can hear bushes scraping on the underside of the car. I look up and Jordy's sitting properly in the seat again. I sit up. Rub the indents from the cans out of my knees. I suck my bloody cheek.

Where are we? I say.

The truck lights the scrub ahead. But around the pool of light everything else is darkness. We're driving straight into the desert.

It's okay, Nev says. It's okay, we've just taken a detour.

But the police were there, I say.

Be quiet, he says.

Kangaroos appear out of nowhere, their fur is ghost white in the headlights. They all stop and look at us. They have beau-tiful long eyelashes. Nev slams on the brakes and I fly forward. I feel my head crack against the glass. At the same time there's the dull sound of kangaroo flesh hitting metal.

Stop it, stop, stop, stop, stop, says Jordy. You're a psycho.

It's going to be okay, Nev says.

Stop the truck, says Jordy.

Nev says, I'm taking you home.

Home? says Jordy. Fuck you.

Just be quiet, he says. But he stops the truck.

Did we hit a roo? I say.

Yeah, says Jordy.

The engine is still running. I touch my head. There's an egg lump. It's the size of my palm. Nev cracks his door and gets out. I hear the scrape of the spade as he gets it from the back. The sound makes me shiver. He's lit red by the truck's backlights. He's a tall man.

Jordy opens his door, but I grab his arm.

Don't, I say. He shakes me off. There is nothing for me to do but slide out as well. I run after him, holding my head egg in my hand.

Is it dead? Jordy says.

Nev is there with the spade in his hand. He looms over the kangaroo and over us. I look up at his red face. It's splattered with blood.

It is now, he says.

I step closer to Jordy. I can feel the nervous heat of us. I look down at the roo, and apart from a severed head it looks perfect, unharmed. I didn't think a spade could be so sharp. I touch the pelt. It's warm and soft. I look up at Jordy.

Check its pouch, Jordy says. I pat its front. I can feel the hard muscle beneath the fur.

I don't want to, I say.

Come on, he says. He gets down with me and reaches into the skin at the kangaroo's belly. It's okay, he says, it's empty.

I pat the roo. I can see the glow of the campground.

You done? We haven't got all night, Nev says.

I hate you, Jordy says to him.

I shrink away from them and Nev leans down. Light glints off the spade. He looks like he's going to backhand Jordy. But he grabs him under his arm and pulls him up to him.

You have ruined everything, says Nev right into Jordy's face.

What. Ever, says Jordy.

Nev throws him back to the ground. He's so tall above us, the spade in his hand. We're down there with the dead roo and the metallic smell of blood.

Get in the truck, he says. Walks away, dragging the spade behind him. I don't know, but I think he's crying.

We could run, Jordy? He looks at me and looks away.

Don't be stupid, he says.

We get in the truck. Nev puts the car into gear and drives forward. The bushes start up their scraping. I look back through the rear-view mirror. The camp glow is gone. The truck nudges its nose back onto the road. Nev heads towards the highway. We have done a large loop through the brush.

I'm thirsty, I say. I hear Jordy sigh and no one answers me. I can see Nev's hands shaking as he changes gears and in between he rests his palm in his lap, a useless thing.

Where are we going? I say.

Button your mouth, Nev says.

I look out at the black. The stars turn on one by one.

Nev pulls back into the roadhouse. When the car stops I can see all the dead bugs splattered on the windscreen. The crack in the windscreen is much larger. Its tail is reaching towards the windscreen edge. Nev pulls up at the petrol pumps. He steps out and stumbles. He steadies himself on the side of the truck and unclicks the handle of the pump. He's humming. I feel every single muscle in my body tighten, from my little toe right the way to the top of my head. I try to relax them. I hear the petrol click full.

Nev gets back in the truck. I can see the muscles in his arms straining to pull himself up into the seat. He rests his hands on the steering wheel. Turns the ignition over. He doesn't go back out onto the highway, though, he parks the car out the front of the roadhouse.

Come on, Nev says. Walks around the hood and pushes the glass door of the roadhouse open. He holds it open for me. It's bright in there. I wait for Jordy. I smell the rot of the gummy on us. There's the same girl there at the counter. I stand behind Nev in a line. I feel someone standing beside me. I smell watermelon. I look for Loretta's hand. I grab on tight.

Hey there, little fella, she says. I look up and it's not Loretta. It's a girl with sleepy eyes and messy hair. What's up? she says and swings our hands together, smiling at me. I pull my hand away, blushing bright red. I try not to look at her. I hear her stifle a laugh. I look around for Jordy and he's gone too. I try to calm down and look around the room. He's with Nev sitting at a table. They have a two-litre bottle of water between them. Jordy is lifting it to his mouth with both hands. I go over to them. Feel the heat still in my face. I sit in the plastic chair next to Jordy. It scrapes along the ground. I can hear the girl laughing still.

May I have a sip? Gran's politeness slipping out of me. Jordy raises an eyebrow at me and gives me the bottle. Nev has one of the salt shakers in his hand. He's shaking it up and down with his hand over the top so that no salt escapes. I can see little grains of rice in there. My hand on the water bottle is black with dirt. The label on the bottle has a crystal clear waterfall on it. The bottle's cold, beading clean water. I take a long sip and the cleanness of it makes me taste my mouth, which is horrible. The water goes down the wrong way. I cough but force it down. My eyes go red and teary. Jordy reaches to take the bottle from me, but I hold it and pull away. Take another sip.

The bus comes through here in the morning, Nev says.

What do you mean? says Jordy. Nev looks at us and crosses his arms. Jordy says, You can't leave us.

The girl comes over, jolting her hip to the side. The burgers? she says. Nev motions towards us. She leans over and plonks the plates in front of us. Chips spill off the side. Jordy takes a chip and shoves it in his mouth. Chewing loudly. I don't feel hungry at all, but take a bite of my burger. Sauce drips onto my hands.

This tastes disgusting, I say. Nev gives me a disbelieving laugh and shakes his head. I can see tears in his eyes. As I chew I can taste the gummy. I look at my burger and the grey of the meat looks grey as the gummy's skin. I put it back on the plate, pick sesame seeds off the top of the bun. Nev is gripping the edge of the table like it's the only thing holding him up. The air is too cold.

This is all I got, he says. Pulls money from a wallet that's stained by sweat. He tucks the money under my plate. He doesn't look at Jordy.

It should be enough, he says.

You can't do this, says Jordy.

I'm sorry, he says.

He scrapes his chair back and pushes himself up. He walks out of there. I twist in my chair to watch him. He doesn't look back. He gets in the truck, turns north, away from the camp, up the highway.

I feel sick, I say.

Jordy cups his head in his hands over his burger.

The waitress comes over. You kids alright for everything?

We're fine, says Jordy from under his fringe. Thank you. Eat your burger, he says to me.

We sit there until I am done.

I push open the door and walk out towards the pumps. I can hear Jordy behind me shaking twenty-cent pieces in his hand. I walk to the edge of the fluoro light. Out the back of the roadhouse I can see a car doing doughnuts. The headlights making long beams of dust. I can taste the dust. The squeal and rock-pop bangs of fireworks. The sky bursts into colour. It breaks into beautiful pieces. The pieces fade and fall. The car is still there, going round and round in circles. Jordy pulls my arm.

Come on, he says. I grab onto him and he lets me. His skin feels hot. We walk to the phone booth, stuck there in the middle of nothing. He pushes on the glass and the door folds in on itself. The two of us squeeze in.

You do it, says Jordy. He feeds the twenty-cent pieces into the slot. I hear them drop, They like you more, 'cos you're littler, he says. He holds the phone out to me. It's heavy in my hand. He types in the numbers, takes forever. The telephone hums in my ear and clicks loudly with each number. It rings.

Hello, Janice speaking.

Gran? I say.

Love, she says, is that you?

I stare out through the glass blurred by dust. The highway stretches black and liquid into the sky.

ACKNOWLEDGEMENTS

Thank you Caro Cooper, editor at Text Publishing, for doing such a wonderful job. Anna Krien, Benjamin Law, Lorelei Vashti and Kelly Chandler, thank you.